for Mum and Dad, who introduced me to adventures,
and for Arleta, who took this one with me.

THE KNOWN LANDS OF ALTINOR

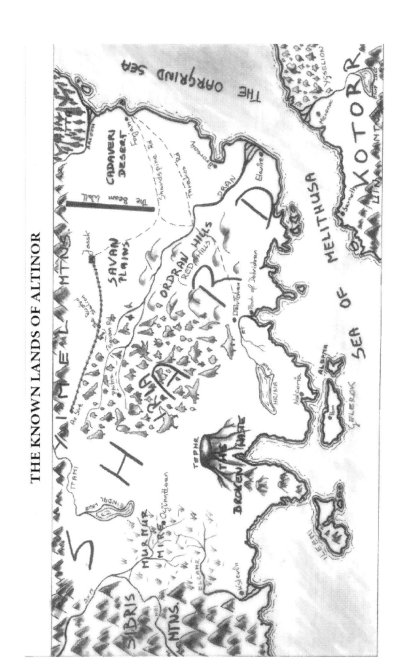

.

CONTENTS

Chapter 1

SCHOOL

Today was another day of staving off boredom. It was a Monday. *Only* four more days until the weekend. Daniel read ahead in his textbooks whenever the teachers began rambling. He read ahead a lot.

During his History lesson there was a section in their books about the Norman conquest of England. Part of the Bayeux Tapestry was on one of the pages. It depicted in an almost cartoonish way a figure in chain mail holding an arrow sticking out of his eye next to a fighter falling after being hit by the sword of a mounted cavalryman. In the text below, the author writes: 'The Tapestry is not helpful as a source to determine exactly how King Harold died, as it is not clear which of the two figures attacked is meant to be Harold, or even if both are meant.' *Both.* Getting an arrow in the eye and then being cut down by cavalry is not a great way to go. To be honest, one of those ways to die would be more than enough. *Did the Normans get to Scotland?* He flicked through the pages but there was no mention of it.

At lunch Daniel sat with Rob, Dean and Jamie. The usual suspects. Sometimes Annabel would join them. Daniel and Jamie teased Rob that she liked him. Annabel was usually chummed along by Katie, who hardly said anything but was always smiling. He wondered if it was a nervous thing.

As they were finishing up and he was about to put his tray away, a boy in their year called Mark, who was a few inches taller than Daniel, tapped Rob on the shoulder.

'Hi Rob, how's things? Not so good I hear,' Mark grinned. Two of Mark's lanky friends, sat at the table he had come from, were watching and sniggering.

'What do you—'

Rob tried to speak but Mark interrupted him.

'You all want to hear something? Something *very* interesting.' Mark pointed his inane grin in Annabel's direction. Poor girl.

'No,' Daniel said.

'Well, I'll tell you ...' Mark said, ignoring him. 'Rob's dad started another bar fight. Again. And lost. *Again.*'

Katie let out a strange squeak of a laugh. Annabel glared at her.

'Get lost, Mark,' Daniel said.

The larger boy pretended not to hear him again and went on.

'Yeah, the Thornhill Arms, wasn't it, Rob? Short, your dad, isn't he? The amount I hear he drinks, he must think he's Mike Tyson before swinging a punch. Too bad it doesn't help him. My mate says his dad was there, and saw his other little embarrassing attempts at throwing a punch before that. Rob's

12

dad went down like a sack of spuds when mine barely touched him. Light as a feather, your dad.'

'Shut up, Mark,' Daniel said.

'Yeah, what's he done to you?' Annabel added.

The larger boy shook Rob by the shoulders and laughed.

'I'm just playing with him, that's all,' Mark said.

'Get off me!' Rob fumed, shrugging off Mark's hands. 'And shut up about my dad.'

Mark leaned in until his nose was inches from Rob's and stared. Daniel thought the vein that often appeared between the spots on Mark's face was going to pop. Unfortunately it didn't.

'I can talk about him however I like. What are you going to do about it?' Mark smirked.

Rob looked at Annabel and Katie, then the boys.

'Come on,' Mark said, 'let's see what you can do. It can't be as bad as your dad. Then again, you do look like him, so maybe you'll punch like a girl too.'

Rob hesitated, torn.

'Don't listen to him, Rob,' Daniel said. 'Mark's *so* tough he feels he has prove it to everybody.'

'I ... I don't want to fight,' Rob said, his eyes on the girls.

'Wee man,' Mark glared at Daniel. 'Was I talking to you?'

In a flash, the bully gripped the back of Daniel's neck and pushed him downwards against his tray, the dirty plate staining Daniel's white school shirt. The girls screamed.

13

'Get off me! Get the hell off!' Daniel shouted, trying to wrestle free.

Jamie, Dean and Rob jumped up at once to pull Mark off Daniel. Mark was thickset and even the three of them were struggling to get him off him.

'See you, Jamie,' Mark said, still pressing Daniel down against the dirty tray, 'your dad doesn't even drink, and you don't even have a dad, do ye, Danny boy?' he smiled. 'Cheat on your mum then leave, did he? He did,' Mark's voice feigned surprise. '*Didn't he?*'

Daniel felt a cold, white rage shooting through his body. He pushed up against Mark's hand with all the strength in his body, spun out of his grip, dodged the bully's grasping fingers and grabbed Mark by the throat with both hands. Daniel squeezed as hard as he could, blind with anger. Mark, trying to speak, managed land a kick in Daniel's stomach. It winded him a moment, but Daniel kept his grip. A courgette slice slid off his shirt onto the floor.

'Daniel, you're choking him!' Annabel said.

'Daniel, stop!' Katie squeaked. 'You'll get in trouble.'

All the children at lunch were now watching. Teachers were running over from the other end of the canteen.

Rob, Jamie and Dean leapt in to pull Daniel off of the bully. Mark was gurgling and kicking more wildly, his face going red. Daniel still held on, though.

'Get *off* him, Daniel, *now!*' His History teacher, Mr

Douglas rushed towards them.

'Daniel, let go, mate,' Jamie said calmly.

'Daniel! What are you doing!? Leave him alone!' a familiar voice shouted.

Daniel turned to see the voice's owner in the crowd; his sister. Rachel looked so innocent. She always looked like that. But she was scared too. He released his grip. Mark, who had been flailing his legs around trying to land another kick on Daniel, fell back on a chair, gasped for air and rubbed his throat with a hand.

'What is the meaning of this? Jamie, Mark, Rob, Dean, and you, yes, you Daniel, you're all coming with me.' Mr Douglas grabbed Daniel's arm and Jamie's and pulled them through the parting crowd towards the canteen doors.

Another teacher, Mr Jefferies gripped Mark and Rob by the arms and followed Mr Douglas and the other boys through the crowd.

'Truth hurts, don't it Daniel?' Mark sneered.

'Pipe down! And it's "doesn't", *not* "don't",' Mr Jefferies said with no hint of sarcasm, wrestling Mark through the crowd.

'Dean Paterson! If you do not follow us,' Mr Douglas boomed, 'there will be a far worse punishment for you.'

Dean sighed and rolled his eyes but followed them out of the canteen.

Daniel was hunched over on the seat in his bedroom, unsmiling.

'Daniel, we talked about this!' his mum said, worried. 'If someone tries to provoke you, just ignore them. Don't allow them to make you angry.'

'He grabbed my neck and pushed me onto my dirty lunch plate!' Daniel flared. 'He was also slagging off Rob and his dad.'

'I don't care whom he was insulting. Mark was wrong to do that, but you were also wrong to attack him. This is not right. For god's sake, Daniel, you could have seriously hurt him! I talked with Head Teacher Ferguson. The school gave you an official warning. You were lucky you were not suspended for this. Two weeks' litter pick as a punishment seems far too lenient for me.'

'Come on, Mum, it wasn't that bad!' Daniel exclaimed, though in his rage he had not felt so sure. 'Only scare him so he wouldn't pick on us anymore,' he continued. 'When he was holding me down, he said father left because he was cheating on you.'

He never called his father 'Dad'. Mum was silent a moment. She then knelt and placed her hands softly on his shoulders.

'Daniel,' she began. 'I know it's really hard for you and Rachel living without your dad being here. It doesn't mean he doesn't love you both.'

'Then why doesn't he *ever* come and see us!'

Daniel's face flushed red.

'Oh, my darling boy, I told you ... He can't. Not right now. I'm so sorry. I hope one day he can visit you and your sister. Really I do.'

'Why can't we see him *now*?' Daniel roared, his brown eyes glassy.

His mum didn't answer at first.

'I'm sorry, Daniel. He's not around. In fact, I don't know where he is.' His mum raised her arms. 'Give me a hug.' Her smile hid that she was sad.

Daniel wrapped his arms around Mum, holding her tightly, as much out of anger as love. *Whatever happened, it wasn't her fault*, Daniel thought. *Or was it? Mum told him his father left them at the time when Rachel was only a few months old. He did not remember him. He remembered asking Mum about his father, but she never wanted to talk about him. Was there something he did wrong, to make him leave?*

'Okay, my darling, listen to me now, we have to keep moving on, no matter what happens, and no more reacting like that, no matter what people say.' Mum's eyes were watery. She pulled herself to her feet, letting go of him. 'I have to check on your sister and make dinner. Tidy the room and do your homework. Then write about how you could handle a situation like that differently next time. I'll be checking later.'

Daniel thought Mum was going to say no TV for weeks like she usually did, but this time she told him to write something. That was different. Daniel knew he had gone too far, but some things just made his blood boil. Once he had finished tidying his room, Daniel took out the school books that were in his backpack and started on his History homework. He preferred writing in pencil; using a pen or typing on a keyboard felt somehow less organic.

He wasn't looking forward to two weeks of litter picking. Rob, Jamie and Dean got a week. *It wasn't fair on his friends.* Despite Mark's plea of innocence, he got two weeks' litter pick too. *I have been put in the same litter pick group as Mark,* Daniel sighed. *Talk about rubbing salt in the wound.* The first litter pick was after lessons the next day. Daniel had been put on litter pick a couple of times before, and recognised some other "repeat offenders". Clasping large black bin bags they scoured the classrooms, corridors and break yard picking up litter and emptying waste-paper baskets. All under the watchful eye of the strict, grammar-obsessed Mr Jefferies.

A few days later, during lunch break, Daniel went to the toilets, leaving his schoolbag against the cubicle in the corner. Mark walked in while he was taking a pee.

'Ah, haha, Daniel ma boy, how's things? That litter pick is completely annoying, ain't it?' Mark made a stupid grin like

18

a cat that had got the cream. Daniel zipped up and moved from the urinal to the sinks. He turned an ancient tap. 'Even more annoying is how you caused it.' Mark stepped towards him.

'I didn't cause it. You did by trying to show off in front of Annabel.'

Mark was next to Daniel's schoolbag. As Daniel went to grab it, Mark tripped him. Daniel tried to balance himself with one arm on the cubicle wall but Mark grabbed his other arm and pushed him down into the cubicle.

'What are you doing? You bastard!' Daniel shouted in pain and struggled to get free.

'Not so brave now, eh?' Mark growled. 'You're a loser, just like your dad.'

'That's a lie!' Daniel shouted, thrashing about, trying to get out of the bigger boy's grip.

'Face it,' Mark said, plunging Daniel's head into the toilet bowl.

Daniel tried with everything he had to get up, but Mark was too strong this time.

'This should teach you a lesson not to mess with me.'

Mark pulled the toilet flush. The stream of water made Daniel choke. He bumped his head against the ceramic pan, trying to push back against Mark's hands.

Mark let go of him. Daniel spluttered, unable to stand for a moment.

'Who's stronger now?' Mark said. 'If you tell anyone, I'll make sure your sister gets the same treatment. See you in lessons, loser.'

Looking down, Daniel heard Mark throw something in the bin and leave the toilets. Daniel punched the cubicle wall. Again. Again and again, until his knuckles ached. He wanted to cry. Next time he'd be ready to fight back. He got up. Daniel found his schoolbag in the bin. He cleaned himself and his bag as best he could, and, feeling humiliated, went to his next lesson. English.

Chapter 2

AWAKENING

It was the Sunday after Daniel's two weeks of litter picking. If he didn't have to pick up another wet tissue paper or chisel chewing gum off surfaces for the rest of his life, he'd be thankful. Head teacher Ferguson had warned Daniel and Mark in particular that another misdemeanour would lead to suspension or possible expulsion. Thinking of Mark reminded Daniel of his own head in a toilet bowl. He wished Mark would get expelled. He sighed and looked up at his mum and sister then back at his plate.

Daniel did not want to eat his greens. While his mum wasn't looking, he pushed the cabbage to the side of the plate with his fork, trying to make the pile appear smaller for when she checked.

'Daniel, stop trying to make the cabbage look smaller and finish it,' his mum said.

How had she seen?

'Do I have to? I don't like cabbage.'

'It's good for you.'

'I don't want to.'

'Come on, Daniel. If you eat it all, I have something special for you and your sister.'

'Yeah, come on, Daniel,' Rachel squeaked. 'I love surprises and Mum has the best ones.'

Ever-irritating, Rachel never had a problem with cabbage. Once more, he considered the greeny-white heap on his plate. Rachel was a goody two-shoes, but Mum did surprises well.

'Could you pass the water, Mum?' he said, thinking he could swill down the cabbage with it.

'*Please*,' His mum said, eyes narrowing.

'Please,' Daniel said.

She passed him the water jug and he filled his glass. His mum and sister watched him. After a few moments turning forkfuls of his vegetable nemesis around in his mouth and gulping them down with water, Daniel had made the pile disappear.

'Well done, Daniel,' Mum said.

'Cabbage doesn't taste bad,' Rachel said, grinning stupidly.

'Daniel, take the plates to the sink please.'

He slowly got off his chair, slid his mum and Rachel's plates onto his, placed the cutlery on the top and took them to the sink. He gave them a rinse and put them in the dishwasher.

'Daniel?' his mum said.

'Yep?'

'I'm proud of you for the way you kept your head down

and completed your punishments. I hope you have learned something from them and our talks,' Mum said, eyes widening seriously. Her nostrils flared when she did that.

Daniel made a begrudging nod.

'Now, guess what I have for you both?' Mum said.

'Ice cream? Or even better, a puppy?' Rachel exclaimed.

'I'm pretty sure us getting a puppy would not be dependent on me finishing some cabbage, Rachel.' Daniel chuckled.

'No, not a puppy.' Mum smiled. 'Your favourite. Pancakes.'

'Yay, pancakes!' Rachel squealed with delight, bouncing in her chair.

'Thanks, Mum,' Daniel said, smiling.

'You're very welcome. I know how much you both like pancakes so I thought we could have them for dessert. Lay some fresh plates and cutlery on the table and I'll whip them up.'

Daniel did as she said while watching her mix the ingredients in a large bowl. At the same time he sat back on his chair, Mum placed in front of them some slices of lemon on a small plate, a pot of sugar with a teaspoon sticking out of it and a jar of chocolate spread. Daniel's mouth started watering as Mum brought the frying pan over to the table, in which a large pancake sizzled. Using a pancake flipper, she slid it onto Rachel's plate with a 'Here you go, darling' and turned back to the stove.

'What about me?' Daniel exclaimed. 'How come *she* gets the first one?'

'Come on, Daniel, don't start that again. I'm making yours now,' his mum replied.

'I *am* the oldest,' he said, irritated.

'Daniel, we've been over this before,' Mum said. 'You're a big boy, you can wait a little longer.'

'That's not fair,' Daniel said.

'Come on, you're 11 years old, Daniel,' Mum replied. 'Surely you can wait a few more minutes?'

As he watched his sister take a slice of lemon, squeeze its juice over the pancake and sprinkle some sugar with the teaspoon, he grew even more annoyed.

A few minutes passed before his mother came over with the frying pan in which lay an enormous sizzling pancake. She shuffled it onto his plate with an 'Enjoy' and kissed him on the forehead. *I'm three years older than Rachel, but Mum always puts her first*, Daniel thought angrily.

He reached up to touch the metal symbol hanging from the chain around his neck, which dangled over his chest. It had been a gift from Mum; she said it was for good luck.

Pancakes *were* his favourite food, but the half-eaten one he had smothered in chocolate spread now seemed less appealing. Nevertheless, Daniel ate the rest of it out of politeness and repeated his thanks to Mum as she fried a pancake for herself and set it on her plate on the table. As usual, Mum went through her cleaning routine: she always tidied up the kitchen worktops before sitting down to eat. He asked to leave the table. On hearing a yes, Daniel got up, rinsed his plate and cutlery, put them in the dishwasher and went upstairs to his bedroom.

The street lamps had started to come on, their orange glow cutting through the twilight. It was Monday tomorrow. *School.* He sighed. Every weekday Mum drove Rachel and him in the car to school. It was only a few hundred yards from their home, but Mum liked to make sure they got there on time. She then drove to the nearby town of Dumfries, where she worked at a university library. Mum had given him a pair of house keys; on the rare occasions she had to stay longer at work, Daniel was in charge of getting Rachel and himself home safely after school. This year was his last, Primary 7. Then he would be going to secondary school somewhere else. He wasn't looking forward to the change.

Daniel's thoughts turned to his father. He had no memory of him. His mum had told him that he left them a few months after Rachel was born. He clenched his fists.

Daniel was unsure how long he had been staring out of the window. He went to his mum's room. The bed was made and everything in its place. The door of her reddish-brown wardrobe was open. Inside, Mum's clothes were hanging in perfect order. Below the various trousers, tops, skirts and dresses were her pairs of shoes, in a line and equally spaced. *Why does everything have to be so neat and tidy all the time?* He sauntered back to his room and lay down on the bed. It was not long before he drifted off.

'Daniel? Daniel? Wake up. Don't sleep in your clothes.'

His eyes opened as someone shook him gently.

'You have school tomorrow,' the blur of Mum said as he groaned, 'put your pyjamas on and go and brush your teeth. I checked your alarm is set for 7 a.m. I'm going to bed. Rachel is in her room ready for sleep already. Goodnight.'

She kissed him on the forehead and left the room. Daniel looked at his watch. 21.12. He lifted himself up with his arms but felt so unusually tired, he let himself fall back onto the bed.

'Wake up, Daniel.'

He woke with a jolt. It wasn't his mum talking. Daniel looked around the room. Not Rachel either. He peered out of the window. It was still night, the only breaks in the darkness coming from the stars and the orange glare of the street lamps.

'Daniel.'

He heard it again, a whisper. It definitely didn't sound like Mum, or his sister. *I must be dreaming.* His watch read 00.07. He was still in yesterday's clothes.

'Daniel, come here.' It was a man's voice, deep and a little louder this time, though still barely audible.

He got out of bed and went over to the door. Opening it, he peered round, but the landing was empty. Tiptoeing past his sister's bedroom, all he could hear was her loud snoring. He always wondered how someone so small could make so much noise.

Then it came again.

'I know about your father,' the voice said.

The words startled him. *What do they know about my father?* There was something odd about them, other than the distinctly eerie fact he couldn't see their owner. Muffled, it was as if they were being spoken through a pane of glass.

The voice wasn't coming from his mum's room, which lay silent as he crept past. *They must be downstairs.* Though he wondered how he could hear such a faint voice from so far away. *I must be going mad.*

Daniel crept down the stairs. No one in the kitchen. He checked the other rooms, and in the living room he stopped and stared into the blackness of the TV, having pride of place near the sofa. He spent many Sunday afternoons watching old films with dinosaurs, explorers, flying saucers and screaming passers-by, all accompanied by dramatic music. Rachel always pleaded with Mum to get him to turn down the volume.

He went into the front room, which was never used

except at Christmas and for dinners when his mum's friends came round. Mum's brother, Uncle James, and his wife Aunt Laura, rarely visited and he had never met either set of his grandparents. His mum said they lived abroad, and she never talked about them. But if they ever did come to visit, the front room would be where they'd have tea.

'I'm outside. Come on, don't be afraid,' said the voice.

'I'm not afraid,' Daniel replied.

Back in the hallway, he pulled open the drawer of the hall table, took out a torch that lay next to the spare door keys and switched it on. Grabbing his shoes from their position next to those of his mum and sister by the front door, Daniel put them on and took his coat off the peg. He picked up Mum's ash hiking stick for good measure, removed the door chain, and with a click of the nightlatch and the key in the mortice lock he opened the door.

'Come outside, I'll tell you about your father,' the voice said.

Daniel wondered who the owner of the voice was, and felt it irresponsible and a bit scary to be leaving home in the middle of the night, but curiosity got the better of him. He locked the door behind him. He felt the cold air of the night and zipped up his coat. Nothing moved on the street. Suddenly, a dog, a black-and-white border collie, ran along the pavement. It stopped in front of Daniel, its eyes reflecting the torchlight. Where is its owner? he thought. Hesitating a moment, the dog then darted down the street and disappeared out of sight. Silence. Was someone really speaking to him, or was his mind just playing tricks? He was about to give up and go back inside when the voice returned.

'The park. You will find me there.'

It was as if it travelled to his ears on the breeze.

'Wait a minute, what is all this about? Show yourself!' Daniel said, frustrated.

Silence.

'Tell me!' Daniel said, as if to the air.

Nothing. Cold and annoyed, Daniel made his way down the street to the park's entrance, a hundred feet or so from his house. He entered through the gate in the spiked fence, and soon reached the playground and oval green field, grey and black now in the dim moonlight. The light wind pushed leaves across the paved path that lined the field.

'Go down the path,' the voice said.

He followed the route through the darkness, his torch lighting the way. He checked his watch again. 00.34. Ahead were two tall birch trees, one on either side of the path. He shone the torch up to where the branches met high above him.

'Where are you?' Daniel asked.

'Not far. Walk between the two birch trees,' the voice replied.

'Oh so you *can* hear me! Why are you hiding?' Daniel

said, exasperated.

Why he had not seen anyone so far, however, remained a mystery. He started to feel more scared, thinking leaving the house alone was not a good idea. He gripped the hiking stick tightly, ready to strike.

A rustling sound in the bushes to his left made him jump and he shone the torchlight towards it, raising the hiking stick. He heard a bark, and then noticed the same dog he had seen outside his home. It did not run away this time.

'Hello, what are you doing scaring me half to death?' he said, approaching it.

The dog stared at him past the torchlight. Daniel thought it well looked-after, judging by the sheen of its fur. But it wasn't wearing a collar.

'Have you been following me? Don't you want to be stroked?' he asked as the dog panted, moving away when Daniel stepped closer to it.

Daniel looked back towards the trees. He could hear nothing but the dog moving about and the rustling of leaves in the wind. He passed under the branches of the birches and continued along the path for a few seconds when a blue light appeared. Out of nowhere. He blinked and saw that it was in fact a small blue-edged circle, about three feet in diameter, suspended in the air at chest height a few feet in front of him. Within the circle was the deepest black that he had ever seen, a nothingness that was cold, yet inviting.

Daniel found himself stepping forwards to have a closer look, but before he could reverse this action, the blue ring expanded around him, crackling and flickering with jolts of electricity, and the black hole within it took him. With a loud clap like thunder, he vanished, the torch dropping onto the path, lighting up nearby trees.

Chapter 3

ALTINOR

Daniel woke to darkness. A thumping headache accompanied the pain in his legs. He felt a wetness wrapping around his body. It was his coat. Daniel gripped his arm. The coat was wet and felt caked with mud. His chain was still around his neck. He got to his feet with a groan and removed it, throwing the coat onto the cold floor. His body felt heavy, as if he had grown a lot bigger while asleep. Once Daniel's eyes had adjusted to the gloom, he saw metal bars running from floor to ceiling a few feet from him. Above him was an opening in the roof providing the only source of light. He strained to look at his watch. It had stopped. Beads of water blurred the digital face, but he could make out 00.41. Mum's hiking stick was gone.

Daniel approached the bars and tested their strength with his hands. A gleam of light caught his eye. It came from an opening above another cell to the left of his. Daniel peered through the gloom. Among the shadows, slumped over at the back of the cell was a figure. From what he could make out, they seemed to have more of a scowling mask than a face.

A sudden pain in Daniel's head made him drop to the floor. Through agony like a knife entering his skull, he heard a sound. He summoned what remaining strength he had to raise his eyes and look towards the door to his cell. Through the bars Daniel saw a light. A flame coming down what looked like steps. He glimpsed the outline of the figure carrying the flame. At the bottom of the steps, they stopped and fixed the flame to the wall. Daniel dragged himself closer to the cell bars, his eyes adjusting to the light. The image became clearer. It was a woman, tall, with a dour expression on her face. She wore grey armour, dark trousers and a helmet with a black plume that fell across her upper back. A glint of light flashed into Daniel's eyes. She was holding a spear.

'Get up!' she demanded.

Despite the excruciating pain in his head, Daniel pulled himself to his feet.

'Name?' she asked.

'Why should I tell *you*?'

'You are a prisoner here. It would help you to play along. If you lie, we will torture you.'

'*Torture*?' Daniel said, shocked. 'Where am I? Why am I in this cell?'

'You are here to answer questions, not ask them. Speak, boy!'

'My name is Daniel, Daniel Mearns.'

'Where are you from?'

'Closeburn, Dumfriesshire.'

'There is no place of that name on Altinor, unless it is so insignificant it is not worth knowing.'

'Altinor? I'm from Scotland, the UK.'

This did not seem to register with the woman.

'United Kingdom? Great Britain?'

Nothing.

'Europe?' he continued.

Silence. Daniel was confused.

'You know, on *Earth*,' he said as a joke.

Daniel thought he saw the woman raise an eyebrow and widen her eyes under the helmet, but he could not be sure. She moved towards the bars, producing a key. With a click, the cell door flung open. The woman entered the cell.

'What am I doing here? Daniel said, his voice wavering. *The door is still open*, he thought.

'You are to have an audience with the king,' the woman said.

'What king? We have a Queen in the UK. Who are you?' Daniel said.

She approached with a pair of metal shackles. *Now's my chance*, he thought. *I'll go for the stairs.* Daniel darted for the steps. Before he reached the cell door, he fell forwards, a throbbing pain in his shins, and scraped his knees on the cell floor. Daniel looked back at the woman. She pressed the butt of her spear into his lower back. Before he could struggle, the woman grabbed his hands and forced the metal shackles onto them. Their edges dug into his wrists as she fastened them with bolts.

'Oww! What are you doing to me?' Daniel cried, fear and anger coursing through his veins.

'Quiet!' the woman shouted. 'Up that staircase. Move!'

She aimed the metal spearhead at his back.

Past the door was a hallway where great stone arches curved inwards to form a long pointed roof. On each side were several unlit candles in sconces and doors of different heights with varying styles of handle. He appeared to be in what looked like some sort of castle or fortress.

'Forward!' the woman shouted, prodding Daniel in the back with the butt of her spear.

He continued down the hallway, the chain connecting the shackles around his wrists making a monotonous clinking sound.

After a short time, they stopped in front of a large black metal door reinforced with bolted plates of a duller metal.

'Speak only when spoken to by the king,' the woman said. 'Address him as Your Majesty at first, and thereafter, sir.'

'Why? He's not *my* king.'

Daniel felt a sharp pain in his side. He realized she had cut him, and that his T-shirt was sticking to his body.

'Do not provoke me,' she growled.

Daniel said nothing more. *I have to figure out a way to*

get out of here, he thought, terrified.

The woman knocked on the door three times with the butt of her spear. Daniel was telling himself not to be afraid, but the clangs of wood on metal sent a shiver down his spine. He wondered about the king, hoping he would be more approachable than the woman.

The knocking received no reply. After a few minutes, Daniel heard a click as another door opened behind them, then footsteps. They turned to see a short man walking towards them. Like the woman he held a spear and wore dark grey armour and a helmet, though his had no plume at the back.

When the figure was closer, Daniel could see it was in fact a boy not much older than himself. On the boy's bare right wrist was a barcode lit up in green, and below it shone a large digital display of green numbers. The boy looked as if he wanted to say something. The woman peered down at him, and the boy soldier stopped, clicking his boots to attention. The boy bowed his head for a moment.

'At ease, Private,' the woman said.

'Captain,' the boy addressed her, spreading his feet apart and placing his hands behind his back. 'I have been ordered to inform you that His Majesty commands you be present during the interrogation.'

Interrogation, Daniel thought, worried.

'Private, inform His Majesty we are ready at his

36

convenience.'

'Yes, Captain.'

The boy scurried off through a small door in the wall adjacent to the metal door and left it open, allowing a gust of wind to blow into the room. Daniel felt the cold air on his cheeks. Then the door slammed shut, the noise echoing down the hallway. With a mechanical clanking sound, the shiny black door opened like a portcullis.

'Approach!' a gruff voice ordered.

The captain prompted him with a prod, her face expressionless. The room beyond was just as Daniel would imagine throne rooms to be in fantasy stories: a king, seated on a throne raised above the floor, guards stationed to either side of the great chair, wide stone columns holding up a colossal roof. All around the room large candles oozing globules of wax as their flames flickered, casting dancing shadows on the walls. The king himself had blond hair, was tall and thickset, his face unsmiling. On his head he wore a gold crown encrusted with diamonds and gemstones of many different colours. A quilted tunic with elaborate embroidery covered his frame, with woollen trousers and stout boots on his legs and feet. He looked around forty years old. Daniel wondered what he would be asked, and what he'd reply. What would his friend Jamie, or Rob, say? He knew what Dean would say. He'd tell the king to shove his questions up his—

'Captain, the name of the prisoner?' the king barked, pulling Daniel away from his thoughts.

'Daniel Mearns, Your Majesty,' the captain replied.

'What brings you to my kingdom, boy?' the king asked.

Daniel took a deep breath.

'I don't know. I woke up in a cell and couldn't remember how I got there.'

'First, you address me as Your Majesty, then sir. I thought you would have been told that.' The king looked at the captain, his eyes narrowing.

'I was,' Daniel replied.

'With your permission, sir, perhaps I can explain?' the captain said.

'Speak.'

'I found the prisoner lying unconscious in a shallow well in the Broken Waste, sir. I instructed my men to lay his body across one of my spare horses and brought him to the castle.'

'What were you doing in the water? Stealing a drink?' the king asked.

He stared at Daniel, unblinking, making him feel very uncomfortable.

'I was not stealing, and I don't remember being at a well! I don't remember anything that happened before ending up in the cell. Where am I? Who are you?!'

'Remember to whom you speak, or I will put this spear through you!' the captain growled. 'You are alive only at the command of His Majesty enthroned before you, King Ordran the Third of Delvidran and the Far Lands. I told you: address the king as His Majesty, and do not speak unless spoken to!'

'It seems you are deaf as well as stupid,' the king said, a flicker of a smile on his hard face. 'You would do well to remember that to me you are no more than a slave.'

Daniel felt helpless. *He is as strict as the captain*, he thought.

'Where are your parents?' the king asked.

'They're dead,' Daniel replied. He did not wish to tell him anything about his family.

'Hmmm, I think you lie, and still no proper address to a king. We will beat that out of you. What is your age?'

'Eleven.'

'You have been sent by Jassk to spy on us and observe what happens here. Is this true, are you a spy, boy?'

'No, I'm not!'

The king's eyes narrowed again.

'Captain, what is *your* view of the prisoner's story?'

'I believe he tells the truth about not being a spy, sir. I do not think he is in the employ of our enemy,' the captain replied.

'Which region do you come from?' the king barked.

Daniel wanted to make it clearer this time.

'A village called Closeburn, in Dumfriesshire, in Scotland, in the United Kingdom.'

'What do you mean by "kingdom"?' the king said. 'I know all the kingdoms on Altinor. There is none by that name. Speak the truth or I will arrange for a special method of torture to have it out of you.'

'*I am telling the truth!*' Daniel exclaimed. 'It's in Europe.'

The king laughed and looked at Daniel as if he was mad.

'The prisoner must have hit his head,' the king said to the captain. 'And where is this "Europe" then, boy?'

Daniel shivered, his mind awash with methods of torture.

'On Earth. Planet Earth,' he replied quickly.

The king raised his eyebrows. He gave Daniel a piercing stare.

'Interesting ...' the king said, the word trailing off as if a trance had gripped him.

Daniel could feel the captain's eyes on him. He turned to look at her face, which was divided by the nose guard of her thick helmet. Her eyes blazed with anger like hot coals. He tried to stop his legs shaking and wondered what he had said to deserve that stare. Being locked in a prison cell for no crime was not a judgement he thought fair in any country. But he was in no country he had heard of.

'You shall be brought before me again, prisoner,' the king said. 'Until then, think carefully about the truth of how you came to be here. Maybe in the cells you will be reminded of your manners when talking to your superiors. Tarban! Get in here!'

'I didn't mean to come here! I don't even know where *here* is!' Daniel shouted.

'Silence!' the captain barked.

The armoured boy emerged from a side door. The soldiers guarding the king shifted in their posts. Daniel could have sworn they were finding something amusing, though they did not go as far as to smile.

'Your Majesty?' the boy said.

'Take the prisoner back to the cells. I trust you will be able to manage that?' the king said in a sarcastic tone.

'Yes, sir,' the boy replied.

The boy placed a hand firmly on Daniel's shoulder and turned him around. Daniel flashed an angry look at the king while being escorted towards the metal door of the throne room. At the door he glanced back again saw the king talking to the captain. He wondered what they were saying. Daniel decided to try to engage the boy in conversation on the way back to the cell to obtain more information.

'Aren't you a little young to be a soldier?' Daniel asked.

'Quiet!' the boy said.

'Shouldn't you still be in school? I'm in school, Primary 7. How old are you?'

'*School*? What is this school you speak of? Delvidran guards are selected for training at fourteen years old. I am fourteen and left private tuition to become a castle guard. The king is my cousin. He talks about Earth a lot, ever since—'

Daniel dashed back towards the end of the hall, looking for an exit.

'Hey, stop!' the boy shouted, running after him. 'Halt, prisoner!'

To the left of the throne room entrance was a small wooden door. Daniel put his weight against it, and felt it budge a little.

'Stop him!' another voice yelled.

Daniel glanced over his shoulder to see the captain rushing through a doorway behind him to the right of the throne room entrance. He pushed frantically against the heavy door, expecting a spear-thrust to his back at any moment.

The door suddenly gave way and he fell through, but nothing lay beyond it except a crumbling balcony and a sheer drop of a hundred feet or more. Daniel faltered, lost his balance and slipped. He tumbled through the air towards the ground below. *Was this it? Would he wake up now?* He screamed.

Chapter 4

MEETINGS

As he opened his eyes, Daniel saw a large bay-coloured horse drinking water from the castle's moat. It looked up and watched him coughing and spluttering. Daniel struggled to stay afloat due to his hands still being shackled together. It trotted along the bank until it was directly across from him. Daniel kicked with his legs, heading towards dry land.

'Hey! Horse!' Daniel shouted. 'Horse, horse-y! Stay!'

'I don't intend on moving,' the horse replied.

'Wha—you can *talk*? Horses can't talk!'

'We can do many things, including things that children cannot do.'

Daniel reached the bank and pushed himself up with his legs and elbows. He lay panting for a few moments.

'This is getting crazier ... a horse that can talk.'

'Never heard of talking horses, why, I believe you to be a bit short upstairs, boy, and judging by those shackles, you are a prisoner of the castle.'

'I am not short upstairs!' Daniel said angrily. 'I *was* a prisoner, didn't you see me jump?'

'That wasn't a jump,' the horse said. 'You fell.'

Daniel looked over at the massive jungle ahead of him,

which seemed to go on and on forever from left to right.

'Where am I? I don't know this place,' said Daniel.

'You are in Delvidran,' the horse said. 'I think the fall must have damaged your head.'

Daniel looked up to where he had fallen from. The grey walls were high, the stone rough and weathered. It looked like the castles he had seen in history books. High above the moat, on the ledge he had fallen from, stood the captain. She appeared to be staring straight at him.

'They'll be after me ... let me get on your back, horse!'

'I do not answer to *horse*. I have a name, you know, a *sacred* name.'

'Tell me when we're past those trees,' Daniel said, trying to jump on the horse's back. This proved impossible due to his shackled wrists.

'What do you think you are doing?' the horse said, rearing up.

'Whoa! Come on, you have to help me!' Daniel said.

'I do not.'

He touched the horse's back with his hands, but to prevent Daniel trying to climb up again, it leaned on its front legs and kicked its back legs energetically.

'Stop kicking and let me on!' shouted Daniel.

No reaction.

'Sir, uh, or madam ... please. Help me. I won't stand a chance if I don't reach the woods.'

44

The horse stopped kicking.

'Madam ... hmmm, better, though still not the correct way to address me. I should be addressed as "Miss". And that is the jungle of Iria, boy, not a wood.'

I've had enough of this, thought Daniel.

'Okay, whatever, we need to go!'

'I do not know you,' she said. 'You could be a wicked boy, escaping Delvidran in the hope of wreaking havoc across the land. Try to think of it from my perspective. If you can. Why should I help you?'

'My name is Daniel, Daniel Mearns. I am not wicked, if you are able to take me on my word. Now, can you let me on your back please? These shackles are making it difficult for me to climb on.'

At that moment he heard the noise of metal creaking. Daniel could see a platoon of guards emerging from the castle's main gate. They turned briskly in formation towards them, marching in double-quick time. Creatures, too tall and wide to be soldiers, followed the platoon.

'*Please* help me get away, and I'll make a statue of you in our back garden in Closeburn. That's if I ever get home.'

The horse started pacing.

'Earth, was it?' she asked.

'Yes. Do you know it? Have you been there? Can you show me how to get home?'

The soldiers were less than three hundred feet away now.

An arrow slunk into the ground an arm's length from them.

'They're trying to kill us!'

'Shut up and get on!'

The horse bent her legs and lowered her body onto the grass, her back now level with Daniel's legs.

'Don't like your tone, horsey!' Daniel said, clambering onto her back.

The horse lifted herself up.

'Well now we are equally insulted. I shall introduce you to someone who has been to Earth. Do not fall off!'

That exact moment reminded Daniel of being in Uncle James' sports car as it roared through Dumfriesshire villages as though in some Anti-Green Cross Code advert. The horse galloped as if propelled by jets. Daniel grabbed tufts of her thick mane to hold on.

The trees grew in size as they neared the edge of the jungle. Daniel glanced back to his left and then right and noticed some arrows that had landed in the ground not far behind them.

'They're still shooting at us!' he shouted as another arrow landed a few feet to their left.

'Hold on tight!' the horse shouted between loud breaths.

They crashed through the trees and Daniel was sure he would slide off. He was pressing his legs to the horse's body as tightly as he could and gripping her mane with his chained hands, but it didn't feel enough to keep him on. *Where was she taking him? Could he trust her?* The lush jungle was thick and hilly but the horse thundered tirelessly along faint paths and over ridges, kicking small clumps of moss into the air behind her.

Daniel looked up at the dark-green canopy, through which shards of light penetrated every few feet. They sped past a clump of tall plants, each nearly the height of Alpona's shoulder. They had long black jaws the shape of a wolf's snout, specked with dots of light shooting through the canopy above. Their snouts remained still as Alpona shot past. *They must be carnivorous.* Daniel shuddered. That or the plants were protecting themselves from being eaten by something even more fearsome. The horse slowed to a canter, Daniel feeling through his legs the strength of her tightened muscles.

'Why are you slowing down?' Daniel shouted.

'We are deeper in the jungle now,' the horse replied.

'How big is this jungle?' he asked.

'Around seven miles from east to west, thirty from north to south,' the horse said, catching her breath.

Daniel laughed to himself. This was so different to anything he had known in Dumfriesshire.

'Are there other animals here that can talk?' Daniel shouted.

'Yes, but you have to know where to find them,' the horse replied, breathless.

'Cool! So are there talking lions and crocodiles?'

47

'What is a lion?'

'It doesn't matter,' Daniel said, shaking his head.

Now having a moment to gather his thoughts, Daniel thought somehow his body felt lighter here. He glanced back again. No soldiers. The humid jungle air was making Daniel's T-shirt stick to his chest. The sheer variety of greens of Iria's trees and bushes and the flowers, red, blue, violet, brown, yellow, black, pink, orange, some in shades of colour unlike anything he had seen on TV, made him feel both lost and excited at the same time.

They passed an enormous tree. It had *several* trunks, which converged into one high above the ground. The tree's black bark made its trunks look like look like the legs of a huge spider. Far above them, Daniel could see its long, feather-like leaves. They were orange. Many other trees, bushes and creepers in the jungle looked very strange.

'Where are we going? What was your name again?' Daniel shouted.

'I did not give you my name. Keep your voice down. We don't want to attract too much attention,' the horse said.

'Why? What's in this jungle?' Daniel said, lowering his voice.

'I am Alpona. Alpona Meithos. You will see where we are going soon enough.'

'My name's Daniel. Daniel Mearns. How much farther?' he asked.

'You ask a lot of questions. It is not far,' Alpona replied.

'The Devirans who put me in prison, do they also know of Earth?'

'It's *Delvidrans*,' Alpona said. 'Please stop talking, you're giving me a headache.'

Daniel, grumpy, fell silent, peering into the gloom of the jungle.

After several minutes Alpona began to slow, her canter turning into a trot. They were nearing a large tree on a hill, its trunk far thicker than those around it. The leaves on its branches were various shades of green. There was a small wooden hut on flatter ground not far beyond.

Alpona strolled around the tree trunk, which contained deep grooves. It looked very old.

On the other side sat a man, propped up between two thick roots at the base of the tree. He had short, dark brown hair and looked around forty years old. He wore a long hooded jacket that was worn but had been mended in places with patches of many greens and browns. The man's boots were caked in mud and moss. His belt had a metal ring on one side from which an old pistol hung suspended, like one Daniel had seen in a museum in Dumfries he had visited with his mum and sister.

'I met a prisoner of the king. He was flopping around in the moat,' Alpona said.

'I wasn't *flopping about* in the moat,' Daniel said. 'I fell in

49

while escaping.'

'Where do you live, boy? Which region?' the man asked.

'My name is Daniel, not "boy". I'm from Closeburn.' After a pause, he added, 'In Scotland.'

No reaction.

'You know, Scotland, part of the UK. United Kingdom,' Daniel continued.

They looked at him blankly. The man glanced at Alpona for a moment, then back at him.

'That's on Earth, isn't it?' the man said.

'Yes, obviously on Earth,' Daniel said in a sarcastic tone.

'Well Daniel, you are no longer on Earth. This is Altinor.' A faint smile broke across the man's face. 'My name is Ketch. Pleased to make your acquaintance.'

'What do you mean I'm no longer on Earth? Where am I?' Daniel said.

'I just said. On planet Altinor,' Ketch replied.

Daniel's stomach tightened.

'I don't understand … what's going on? This must be some sort of a trick! Did you do this? How did I get here?' Daniel said anxiously. 'Is it far away? How can I get home? Mum must be worried sick …'

'It's a bit complicated to get there,' Ketch said. 'I've been before, travelled around it.'

'You've been to Earth?' Daniel said with hope.

'Ketch has been to a few planets,' Alpona said.

'How did you get there?' Daniel asked.

'A door in space,' Ketch replied. 'Some on Earth have technology as advanced as the city of Jassk on our planet,' Ketch said. 'A place called Tokya, if I recall. Others have less than the Phibs or those living in the desert beyond the Beam Wall. How did you arrive at the castle, Daniel?'

'Tokyo,' Daniel corrected. 'They make robots and games and all sorts of things there. I don't know how I got to the castle. The captain told the king she found me lying unconscious in a well somewhere called the Wastes or something. I woke up in a prison cell in the castle today. Where is this "door in space"?'

'And you were brought before the king?' Alpona asked.

'Yeah, just before I escaped and met you. He asked me where I was from. He asked more questions, and looked interested in Earth when I mentioned it. He ordered I be escorted back to the cells. On the way, I took my chance to escape.'

Ketch's face lost its smile, becoming grave.

'Now, if you don't mind, I need to find a way to get rid of these chains,' Daniel said.

'I have something that'll fix that,' Ketch said. 'Hold on a moment.'

Ketch got up and walked over to the hut. Alpona took to munching on a moist clump of tall grass. Soon after, Ketch emerged with a metal hammer and a long, thin piece of metal.

51

He stopped next to a large rock with a sharp edge along the top.

'Place the chain across the edge of the rock,' Ketch said.

Daniel did so gingerly, and after several blows from the hammer, the chain snapped.

'Now we'll get the shackles on your arms off,' Ketch said, handing Daniel the piece of metal. 'Push this under the manacle's hinge. Then I'll strike the hinge with the hammer. Okay?'

Daniel was nervous. *Miss and the hammer will smash my fingers.* He breathed in, and nodded.

'Left first,' Ketch said.

Daniel pushed the piece of metal between the left manacle's hinge and his skin and hoped for the best. Ketch struck one side of the hinge true until the manacle broke open. The right one took a few more hits, but eventually split.

'Thanks,' Daniel said. 'By the way, in one of the cells was someone. They looked like they were wearing a mask. Who is that? Not that I'd know.'

'I don't know, Daniel,' Ketch said. 'Someone the king doesn't want others to recognise, clearly. Makes me curious too.'

'Probably some heir of a piece of conquered land.' Alpona posed. 'Could drum up support among those serving the king who are native to that part of the kingdom.'

'Back in a moment,' Ketch said.

While the man returned the tools to the hut, Daniel massaged the soreness from his wrists.

On Ketch's return, he said, 'No mean feat, escaping Mornaren. The king is a difficult man to deal with. He—'

'He doesn't like people escaping the castle, obviously,' Alpona interjected. She was taking a break from eating the grass.

'I thought *I* was telling this one, *pony*,' Ketch smiled.

'Don't call me pony, *skink*,' Alpona retorted. 'We have to decide what to do with the boy.'

'*Daniel*,' Daniel growled. 'What's a skink?'

'That's largely up to him. Daniel, do you want to travel back to Earth?'

'Of course I do!' Daniel said. 'But how, where are those space doors?'

'You have to create a portal that leads back to your world, which means using a generator.'

'A generator?'

'Yes, a stardeath generator.'

'Star *death*?' Daniel said, confused.

'Yup. We're still working on the name,' Ketch said. 'If you want to get home, we'll go with you to find the generator parts you need.'

'We *will*?' Alpona said.

'Aren't the soldiers going to be looking for me in the jungle?' said Daniel.

'The Delvidrans that march into Iria rarely spend long here for fear that they will never leave,' Ketch said. 'Phibs patrol the jungle constantly and ambush them with flurries of arrows. We try to do our bit, too.' He smiled and patted the pistol at his side.

'Who are the Phibs?' Daniel asked.

'The captain likes to lead sorties into the jungle,' Alpona said, ignoring his question. 'She sometimes brings her favourite toys ... remember those mechas at the gate? Awful things, made from a dark science that melds beings with machines.'

'They are not mechas, Alpona,' Ketch said. 'They are not piloted by conscious beings, but unconscious. Slaves to the king and captain's commands. They are biomechanical monstrosities. You don't want to meet one if you can help it. When the king will want to take Phibia and occupy the jungle, they could win him the battle.'

What the hell have I got myself into? thought Daniel.

'Why do they want to occupy the jungle?' he asked.

'For now, they take rubber sap from the trees,' Alpona said. 'The king wants to expand his territory and find the resources to create a portal to your Earth.'

Daniel blinked.

'He wants to find a woman who lived with him, but left some years ago.'

'Isn't that a good thing, him trying to find her?' Daniel

said.

Ketch sighed, and sat back down between the roots of the great tree.

'He wants to find her for her child. The king made her queen by force.' Ketch gritted his teeth. 'Her family is known across Altinor, as many of her ancestors had an extraordinary characteristic. With only their minds they could create force fields, bubbles of energy around themselves that protected them from any attack, mental or physical. The ability meant they became near invincible warriors. Thankfully, few of them ever lusted after great power or territory, or the whole of Altinor would have been ruled by one family.'

'So can she make force fields? Cool ... How did they stop the few that did want to expand their territory?' Daniel said.

'We do not know. I may have an idea, but can't be sure,' Ketch said. 'The woman's family used the ability to protect their ancestral lands in the mountains beyond the town of Ao Sirt. "The Shields", people called those warriors. She does not share this characteristic. Sometimes this extraordinary gift would skip a generation. Nevertheless, the king believes her child has the power and he intends to raise it himself and control it to help him become the greatest conqueror of his family, the Natos.'

'And you think she went to Earth using one of those stardeath things?' Daniel said.

'Who knows what happened?' Ketch said. 'Excuse me a

moment, I am going to have a brief conversation with Alpona.'

Ketch looked at the horse and indicated with his head where they were going to talk. While they were out of earshot and facing away from him, Daniel crept behind a tree with thick vermilion vines nearer to them to try to hear their conversation. He could just make out what they were saying. He leaned round the trunk and peered between vines to watch, taking care he was not spotted.

'Yes, we *will* help the boy, but only if you don't have any prior engagements eating grass, Alpona,' Ketch said.

Daniel's eyes shifted to Alpona, who moved one of her hooves back and forth against a fallen branch.

'Okay, fine,' she agreed, snorting, 'but I won't be responsible if he dies,' Alpona said. Her ears twitched.

Daniel started to panic. What *exactly* were they going to be doing?

'We'll collect the machine parts and keep a close eye on him. He may prove useful,' Ketch said.

They turned, appearing not to notice that Daniel had been behind a nearby tree and was now pretending not to listen, picking up stick and waving it around like a sword.

'You may need something stronger than that,' Alpona said to Daniel. 'We have decided to help you.'

Daniel wanted to ask something, but felt unsure. His curiosity got the better of him.

'I have something bothering me. One night when my mum and sister were asleep, I was called to a place, a park near my home in Closeburn by a voice that seemed to have no owner, or none I could see. It was a man's voice and it said it knew about my father. I have no memory of my father. My mum left him when my sister and I were very young. Something made me want to see if what the voice said was true. It told me to walk between two birch trees in the park, and a darkness, pitch-black and ringed by blue light, opened around me, the strangest thing I have ever seen. I don't remember anything after that until I woke in the prison of the castle. Have you heard anyone mention having a son called Daniel?'

'I'm sorry, I haven't. We don't have many Daniels on Altinor, if any,' Alpona said. 'I would remember if I had heard the name.'

'Sorry, can't say I have, Daniel,' Ketch said. 'We need to combine various components for the stardeath generator to work, but it should do the trick.'

'How does the generator work?' Daniel said.

'It creates a minute star then uses a form of nuclear fission to cause it to die, creating a black hole. A ring of particles restricts the black hole to prevent it from sucking everything around it into the portal, thus forming a tiny wormhole in space.'

'Don't blow your own trumpet too much, Ketch,' Alpona

said. 'Ayelet came up with that theory.'

'Well, Alpona, you know I supported her theory when I designed the generator,' Ketch said, smiling. However, Daniel thought he could detect a sadness in the man's eyes. 'After use, when the generator is turned off,' Ketch continued, 'the wormhole disintegrates. I think you have them on Earth, too.'

'We *do*? Not that I know of,' Daniel said. 'Then again, I am only eleven.'

'So what do we need to find first?' Alpona said.

'That depends on which order Daniel wants to search for the components,' Ketch said.

'I gave the main box of the generator to Ayelet Szor, whom Alpona mentioned earlier. She is a good friend of mine and a scientist. She discovered the science behind portal generators and wanted the box to conduct experiments. That was about a year ago and I haven't seen her since. Said she was travelling by boat to the port of Forjan, east beyond the Beam Wall. The rubber belt used to drive the machine is in the hands of Phorm Drayd, Lord of the Phibs. He lives in a large village in this jungle, north of here. The last component is a jewel, a green stone I traded for a rare metal with a merchant in Jassk city. Each time the machine is switched on, the stone, when energised by bolts of electricity from the generator, creates the minute star and begins the process of nuclear fission. As you are the one who wants to return to Earth, we leave the order of recovery of these three components up to you, Daniel.'

'*I* decide?'

'Yes. Did you not hear me?' Ketch laughed.

Daniel paused for a moment.

'Why are you telling me all this?' he asked. 'I appreciate you helping me escape from the soldiers and removing those chains, I do, but we've just met. Why are you so quick to want to help me? Why should I trust either of you? What's in it for you?'

'We don't like the king,' Alpona said. 'Helping you return home is a good way to spite him.'

Daniel scrunched his eyebrows together. It did not feel like that was the whole story. He looked at Ketch.

'Plus, we simply don't want to see someone separated from his family by light years,' Ketch said.

'Also, we wouldn't want you to get up to any mischief on Altinor,' Alpona added. She blew air loudly from her nostrils. Daniel found that amusing.

'Okay, I don't know this world,' he said, 'but how can I be sure that you are telling the truth about the generator?'

'Well, it seems you'll just have to trust us,' Ketch said. 'I used to be Collector for Mornaren Castle. King Ordran asked me to hunt far and wide for objects of interest to him, so I know a bit about this kind of science from Ayelet and others, and what it takes for you to return home.'

'A Collector?' Daniel said. 'Of what exactly?'

Alpona looked at Ketch.

'A Collector, Daniel, is similar to what people in your world call an engineer. We create things and keep them running. When I lived in Delvidran, the king also asked me to make things for his military: machines, weapons, things like that.'

'I see. Why don't you live in Delvidran any more?' Daniel said.

Alpona resumed eating grass. She looked up and finished the sizeable clump sticking out of her mouth.

'The king and I had a difference of opinion,' Ketch said curtly. Daniel searched the man's face for a reveal of untruth.

'The Woodsman is correct about the generator,' Alpona said. 'There will be danger during our expedition. Do you believe you are up to it, Daniel?'

'Of course I am!' he replied. 'Woodsman?'

'I am called that sometimes because I live here ...' Ketch sighed.

'Let's visit Phorm ... Phorm and the Phims, was it?' Daniel said.

'Phibs,' Alpona corrected.

'Yeah, them,' Daniel said. 'Let's see them first and get this belt. Which way?'

'You've changed your tune,' Ketch smirked.

'Not at all,' Daniel said. 'I just want to get home before Mum begins to worry,' Daniel said.

'It might take a bit longer than that,' Alpona said, baring an enormous set of yellow teeth.

Chapter 5

PHIBS

'How far is it now, horsey?' Daniel asked from Alpona's back. 'Why are you going so slowly? I know you can gallop faster than this.'

'C'mon horsey, tell us!' Ketch smiled from behind Daniel.

'Address me by my name, or I will buck the both of you from my back,' Alpona said.

'Alpona, Alpona, are we getting close to the village?' Daniel asked. *He didn't fancy walking there.*

'Considering I've been galloping for around half an hour, yes, you could say that.'

'Alpona's gallop is faster than that of most horses, it must be said,' Ketch conceded, 'though I dare say she gets more distracted by grass.'

'That's not true,' Alpona snorted. 'I require more sustenance than other horses.'

'It will be interesting to meet these Phibs,' Daniel said. 'How can we get this rubber belt from the portal machine back? Do you think we can buy it?'

'Phibs don't use currency,' Ketch said. 'Even if they did, I don't think Phorm would want to sell it anyway. Phibs like to barter one thing for another. I went to reason with their leader, Phorm, after he stole it from me, but he did not allow me into the village.'

'He *stole* it from you?'

'Yes, came with some warriors and took it from the hut while I was asleep. He wears it as a kind of symbol in front of the tribe. Despite that, in my experience Phibs are true to their word and sensitive about their honour.'

'We have to get it back,' said Daniel.

'There's a glade up ahead,' Ketch said. 'Let's stop for a while.'

Daniel didn't see why at first, but the loud snorts from Alpona's nostrils made him think it might be a good idea. *But only for a while.*

As they drew up in the glade, the shock of light from above made Daniel squint. Ketch dismounted Alpona, and Daniel did the same. Still snorting deeply, Alpona noticed a large clump of lush grass nearby and lowered her head to taste it. Her whinnies afterwards made Daniel think it must have tasted good. Ketch sat against a nearby tree and removed a pistol from his belt.

'You have these in your world, right?' he said.

'Yes, but that one looks very old. *Museum old*,' Daniel said. 'We have more modern guns than that.'

He remembered reading about the weapons and other equipment of soldiers in a book given to him by Uncle James.

He was often abroad and rarely visited them; he had served in the Army in the Falklands, Sierra Leone and other faraway places that Daniel could not recall. He was pretty sure Uncle James had never been *this* far away, though.

'These flintlocks are what we have developed so far here, and not many of them,' Ketch said. 'Do you know how to load one?'

Daniel shook his head.

'Let me show you. This ... is the pistol cock.'

With his thumb Ketch pulled the gun's hammer back halfway until it clicked. He then tilted the pistol upwards at a 45-degree angle and removed a thin rod from the metal carriage below the gun barrel. He pushed the rod right down the barrel, then pulled it out; *just like in the history films about the American Independence War*, Daniel thought.

'This is to check the barrel is empty,' Ketch said.

He then returned the rod to its original position in the carriage. Producing what looked like a sharp piece of flint from a pouch attached to his belt, he placed it into what Daniel thought resembled two metal jaws on the top of the pistol. Ketch tightened a screw that ran between the jaws to hold the flint in place. He tilted the pistol directly upwards so that the business end pointed into the air, and unclipped a flask from a strap connected to his belt that ran across his chest and over his right shoulder, which held two more pistols on metal rings above several holding flasks.

Ketch tipped a small amount of black powder from the flask into a measurer, and poured the contents down the barrel. He slid the powder down into the barrel with a steady firm push of the ramrod. He then took a piece of wadding made of torn cloth from a second belt-pouch and placed it on the end of the barrel. Removing the ramrod from its holder once more, Ketch used it to push the cloth wadding down inside the barrel, then again to insert a round bullet he had collected from another belt-pouch, joining the powder and wadding in the barrel. He then returned the ramrod to its carriage.

'This is the frizzen,' he said, pointing to an L-shaped piece of steel opposite the metal jaws at the back of the gun. 'We open this ...' He pushed the frizzen away from the cock. '... to reveal the pan.'

Daniel examined the pan. To one side was a small hole in the metal.

'Now we place a quill in the touch hole ... here,' Ketch said, pointing to the small hole to one side of the pistol's exposed pan.

He took a quill with a ring bored into its feather-end from the strap across his chest and placed its nib-end into the hole.

'We put that there to prevent it from filling with powder. And in *this*,' Ketch said, unclipping a smaller flask from the strap, 'is the primer.'

He pushed a lever on the side and filled an attached metal measure with another, more finely ground gunpowder, which he poured into the pan to just under a third of the hole. He took out the quill and wiped any excess away with a piece of wadding. Ketch then pushed the frizzen down over the pan to hold the primer powder in place.

'Now it's loaded and primed. Remember to cock it before you fire by pulling the hammer back ... here,' he said, pointing, 'until it clicks into the position of being fully back, which is full cock. You got it?'

'I think so,' Daniel said, uncertain. 'Can you just show me again?'

Ketch went through the process again.

'Okay,' Ketch said after loading the pistol, 'when you pull the trigger, *this*,' the man said and pointed at the flint, 'hits the frizzen, this bit here, which creates sparks. They hit the primer, the powder in the pan here, and the flash travels into the muzzle, where it ignites the powder pushed into the barrel behind the wadding and the bullet. Then you want to have the barrel pointed only at your target, because that's when it goes off. Or misfires if something's wrong.'

Though he would not admit it, Daniel was rather interested in the process. He had never thought he would see a gun being loaded that looked two hundred years old. Not in his world anyway. He would also never have thought he'd be in a place where that kind of gun was the most advanced they had.

'Why are you showing me this now?' he asked.

'In case I get shot in the village, and you have to take one from my body to defend yourself,' Ketch said.

Daniel's eyes widened.

'Are you expecting to get shot!?'

Ketch did not reply.

'Ok, could you repeat the process one more time please?' Daniel asked, concerned.

Ketch repeated the steps of loading the gun while Daniel focused on every detail.

After that, Ketch unclipped another flintlock pistol from a ring on the strap and handed it to Daniel. Daniel thought it was heavy.

'When I think you're ready,' Ketch said, 'I'll let you carry one of these.'

'The only thing the Phibs welcome is a challenge,' Alpona said through a mouthful of grass. 'If we can think of some way to contest Phorm,' she said, looking at Daniel, 'then we might have a chance of reclaiming the rubber belt.'

'Challenge? This is getting worse,' Daniel said, concerned.

'Except Phorm only accepts a challenge when there's something in it for him,' Ketch said. 'We'll think of something. I have a small machine I think they may find very useful.'

Daniel and Ketch pulled themselves up onto Alpona's back and she began to trot, accelerating to a canter into the intermittent gloom of the deep jungle. Daniel wondered what the people they were going to meet would be like. *They must have young Phibs, too—are they like the boy soldier in the castle, or allowed to play?*

'Alpona, do you think the Delvidrans will return to the jungle looking for us?' he asked.

'I think they may well do, particularly if they know you came from Earth. They will want to examine you further if they catch you again.'

Daniel didn't like the sound of that.

Alpona suddenly picked up her speed, as if she had been surprised by a rider's spur.

'All because I'm from the planet the queen *may* have escaped to?' Daniel said.

'For the king, any link to your world is useful,' Alpona explained. 'He probably thinks he can use you as a guide on Earth once he's found a way to open a portal. He will keep searching until he has found his queen and her child.'

'Don't call her *his* queen,' Ketch said.

'Sorry, Ketch,' Alpona said with some sadness.

'So the king forced her to marry him and called her his queen? That's out of order,' Daniel said.

'You can say that again,' Alpona agreed.

'She was journeying under guard from the castle to Ao

Sirt when she was allegedly abducted en route through Iria. People said she was taken by my scientist friend Ayelet Szor and sent to another world. The king tracked down Ayelet and tortured her until her mind cracked. She confirmed it was true, and that Earth was where she had sent her. We have to stop the king from finding her,' Ketch said.

'Why you?' Daniel asked.

Ketch was breathing heavily.

'Because she is my wife,' Ketch said. 'The king started admiring her. He said he would have me killed if she didn't marry him. To save my life, she did, and the king exiled me from Delvidran a long time ago so that he might have her for himself.'

'Wait a minute! *You* were married to the queen?'

'*Am*. I *am* married to her. Our marriage never ended. The king had me exiled under the pretence of making flintlock weapons for the Jassk military.'

'That's ... horrible,' Daniel said.

'We are outside the village. Stay silent,' Alpona instructed.

'This is Phibia, the ruling village of the Phibs in Iria. Can't say I've missed this place. Let's hope for a better reception this time,' Ketch grinned.

Daniel thought the man's grin looked a bit sour.

From some way off they saw the village gate, in front of which stood a sentry. Daniel was struck by the guard's

69

appearance—he looked like a huge frog, but was tall and stood like a man on its hind legs, holding some kind of a gun in its hands, similar to the flintlocks Ketch carried. He was pretty sure *nowhere* on Earth had massive humanoid frogs that walked on two feet.

'What have you come here for, Woodsman? And who is with you?' shouted the frog.

Daniel and Ketch jumped down off Alpona's back and the three of them walked towards the guard. Daniel thought it strange and amazing that he could understand what the Phib was saying.

'Did you make guns for the frogs ... uh, Phibs?' Daniel asked Ketch.

'Unfortunately, yes, in order to pay for things when I was exiled from Delvidran by the king,' Ketch said. 'It was before Phorm stole from me.'

'The Phibs having guns has so far kept the village free from Delvidran involvement,' Alpona said. 'Though I'm not sure they enjoy using them. They are clumsy weapons.'

'What's that, Alpona?' shouted the Phib, who was now marching towards them. 'Don't think I'm averse to using mine if I find something's not right here.'

Alpona sighed.

'You know each other?' Daniel said in a low voice to Alpona.

'Used to fight alongside him and the other Phibs against

the Delvidrans. Those that tried to take Iria. That was before the Radiants appeared. Be quiet, please.'

As the Phib approached, it became clear that he wore a brown pouch across his body, and his gun was a flintlock.

'Why have you come back, Ketch? You know what Lord Phorm said. I asked you before, who is with you?' said the frog, staring at Daniel.

'He is a friend of ours; we are trying to help him return home,' Ketch explained.

'He is not from around here,' Alpona added.

'We request an audience with Phorm,' Ketch said. 'There is a deal we can offer him.'

'Woodsman, after your last trip here I am sure Lord Phorm will not change his mind,' replied the sentry.

'We have a trade to propose.'

'What is it?' asked the Phib, his enormous, bulbous eyes shining in the beams of light as he stood in front of them.

'That would be telling. Ask your lord if he will see us, and then you'll find out.'

Angered, the sentry shook the pistol a little, cocked it fully and pointed it at Ketch's chest.

'Listen, if you do not tell me what you wish to trade, I will drop you here and take it anyway.'

Ketch didn't move a muscle, but Daniel believed it was from courage, not fear.

'Lokash, you are not a big fish, so why try acting like

one? Phorm decides what happens here, as you well know. If he finds out that you have taken something of value from me and chose not to present it to him, well, let's just say you will soon be begging for as swift a death as a bullet to the brain.'

The Phib stood there for a moment, his black eyes unblinking. He fired out of frustration at the trunk of a nearby tree, causing Daniel to jump in fright. The frog's expression then eased, and he began to laugh insincerely.

'Ketch, c'mon, you know I'm just fooling around. I may be many things, but I am not a thief.'

'I'm not sure that could also be said of his leader,' Alpona muttered to Daniel.

Lokash lowered his gun.

'Now, forget my jesting while I show you to Lord Phorm.'

'Mmm ... though you must make sure we *all* receive an audience with Phorm. If not, I will inform him of your attempts at robbery when on guard.'

The sentry gave Ketch an icy look, and turned back towards the village gates.

'Follow me,' he said. 'Once inside, I will tell Lord Phorm of your presence.'

Lokash brought them before his leader. Outside a huge wooden house, Lord Phorm Drayd sat on a gigantic throne carved into the widest, tallest tree stump Daniel had ever seen. Though seated, it was obvious to Daniel that he was a lot bigger than the frogs gathered around him. Phorm wore no crown, but Daniel could see a flintlock pistol in a holster attached to a belt across one sinewy shoulder, while across the other was a black rubber belt. Several guards stood either side of the throne, each armed with a flintlock pistol and a sharp wooden spear. Daniel thought Phorm looked bored.

'Lokash, why did you let this wretch into our village?' he bellowed down from his throne.

'Phorm,' Ketch said, 'I am not here to quibble over how you got the rubber belt you are wearing. We're here to offer a trade. I have made a rare sun-trap.'

'What good is this *trap* to me? I am not Lord in this village so that I can be deceived by you!'

'The sun-trap is made of korcite,' Ketch explained. 'It collects energy from rays of natural light and converts it into power for electronic devices, such as lamps, cookers and vehicles.'

'I have no use for that!' Phorm laughed. 'Why do you come here with nothing to bargain with? Remove them!' he ordered.

'Wait! The sun-trap can power weapon-makers, too,' Ketch said. 'It would run the machine I left in the village when I made guns for your tribe, if you still have it. And you will need more if you want to resist the Delvidrans.'

'Hmm,' Phorm grunted. 'What do you want in exchange for this machine? No, don't tell me. *This*?'

Phorm gripped the rubber belt across his shoulder and pulled it forwards, letting it snap back onto his chest.

'Exactly,' Ketch said.

'And why do you need *mine*?' Phorm said. 'Why not make a new one?'

'It is not *yours*,' Ketch said. 'And I take it you know that the rubber trees in Iria have been drained by Delvidran rangers of sufficient sap to make another.'

'It *is* mine!' Phorm roared. 'Your own thieving people beat you to the rest of the sap! Who is this, Alpona?' Phorm asked, peering down at Daniel.

Alpona opened her mouth to speak, but was interrupted.

'My name is Daniel, Daniel Mearns. You are a thief as much as the Delvidrans. Give him his belt back. It doesn't belong to you.'

Ketch and Alpona took a sharp intake of breath. Phorm's grin widened, and he moved forwards on his throne to get a better look at Daniel.

'Daniel, eh, boy? Who are you to question my honour? I am the Lord of the Irian Jungle. I'll tell you how you can have it.'

Never taking his eyes off him, Phorm stood up and descended the steps carved into the tree stump. He appeared even larger than Daniel had first thought. Phib guards pressed around Daniel, blocking any escape. They pushed him with their spears towards their lord. Phorm unclipped the flintlock pistol holder on the strap across his shoulder, and let it fall to the ground with a thump. Then the great frog grabbed a spear from a nearby guard.

'Beat me in single combat.'

'That's not fair!' Ketch shouted. 'He's just a boy.'

He and Alpona moved forwards to join Daniel, but they were blocked by Phib warriors' spears.

'A boy who has insulted me. Phibs fight in single combat from when they are young, so will he.'

Daniel's knees were beginning to shake. He hoped the others could not see it.

'This is the way we decide disputes,' Phorm continued. 'We will fight with spears as per tradition. If you win,' the frog lord snorted, 'then I will give you the belt, and following the custom of our tribe, renounce my position as Lord of the Phibs. But if you lose, you will remain our prisoner, the suntrap will be ours, and *you*,' he said, looking at Ketch, 'will teach my frogs how to make guns.'

Daniel wanted to ask if he had a choice, but no words came out.

'Throw him a spear!' Phorm ordered one of his warriors.

One landed at Daniel's feet. This was it, he had to do it. He crouched to pick up the spear, and as he did so the great frog lunged at him. He didn't have time to think, and rolling sideways, Daniel barely managed to evade Phorm's spear. With Phorm advancing, striking high and low, Daniel defended only through instinct. He dodged a rapid succession of attacks by jumping backwards and ducking to one side, but, forced to parry, he lost his footing under the strength of his opponent. He knew he couldn't keep this up for much longer. He rolled again. Phorm's spear fell to the ground with a thud but remained intact.

'Daniel! Aim low! Aim low, son! At his feet!' Ketch shouted, trying to push past the ring of Phib spears around him and Alpona.

Phorm was about six feet ahead of Daniel, swivelling his spear in circles, playing to the gallery. His great webbed unguarded feet seemed the only promising target, but Daniel couldn't find the right moment to strike amidst Phorm's flurries. Phorm attacked again—Daniel ducked the high spear and moved around the great frog's bulk. Phorm's momentum had taken him straight past Daniel and into a tree, his spear embedded in the bark. Daniel moved as quickly as his legs would allow, not to attack Phorm from behind, but to get between him and the tree. As Phorm was trying to pull his weapon free from the tough bark, Daniel knew he was too broad for him to be able to get between him and the tree from the side. Also, the superior peripheral vision of the frog's bulbous eyes (Daniel had read that in his Biology textbook) meant he would spot him.

Starting to run, Daniel leapt up onto the curved back of his opponent, jumping again over Phorm and bringing the butt of his spear down as hard as he could onto the great frog's head. Phorm went crashing to the ground, and Daniel knocked his opponent's spear from his grasp before landing between him and the tree with his spear aimed straight at Phorm's now exposed belly.

'Give up, Phorm,' Daniel said.

Alpona whinnied and Ketch pumped the air with his fist and attempted what could only be described as an impromptu "glory dance", while Phib guards attempted to discourage him. Phorm looked stunned.

'Ah, boy, you have indeed bested old Phorm,' he said, shocked but gracious.

'He's not *that* old,' Ketch told the crowd.

'I accept your victory, according to the tradition of our people,' Phorm said. 'Guards! Lift your spears from his friends. Daniel, let me present your trophy.'

The circle of spears around Ketch and Alpona raised to the sky and the guards let them push past and join him. Daniel took the spear off Phorm's belly and raised it to the sky. The frog leader removed the black rubber belt and passed it to Daniel, who threaded one arm through so that it rested on his left shoulder.

'Now, as promised, I reward you with the honour of the belt I once held. Let my tribe see this act as the renunciation of my position as Lord of the Phibs. In accordance with our laws, we shall hold an election this evening, to choose a new leader to bring honour to the frogs of Iria.'

There was a loud, guttural cheer from the crowd.

'Please, honourable warrior, you and your friends must stay for dinner,' a female frog offered.

'We are sure that it would indeed be a delightful feast, but on this occasion we must say a grateful "no thank you", for we have a long journey ahead,' said Alpona.

'I want to stay,' Daniel said to Alpona. 'Unlike you, I've never had a feast in this forest, and I *am* guest of honour.'

'Trust me, you'll be surprised. It's not exactly what you'd call *cordon bleu*,' whispered Ketch.

Surely any meal after such a victory would taste sweet? Daniel thought.

'Er, it's Plicca, isn't it?' Ketch asked the frog.

She nodded.

'Do you happen to know how far it would be for us to travel to reach the Rusted Station?'

Plicca looked at him for a while in silence.

'A few hours' march,' she said eventually, 'if you take the Savan Road across the river. Are you sure you won't stay for our feast?'

Alpona smiled, exposing her enormous set of yellowing teeth, and shook her mane. The frog turned to pick something flat and green from a barbeque-like fire being watched over by an attending Phib cook.

'Well, at least take some roasted crocus shoots for the

journey,' she said, offering them.

Ketch graciously accepted. He handed one of the huge shoots to Daniel and placed another in front of Alpona's mouth.

'Thank you, Ketch, but I think I'll save it for later,' she said.

Daniel ripped a piece of the leathery crocus shoot with his teeth and chewed it. Bitter and tough, it took a lot of chewing before he could swallow it. He folded the rest of his crocus shoot and placed it in his pocket. Ketch chuckled and folded his own and Alpona's, placing the shoots in one of the large pouches on his belt.

'Thank you, Plicca, and to all of the Phibs,' Ketch said in a loud voice. 'We hope to see you again after our travels, in friendship!'

The Phibs cheered and applauded Daniel and his friends as they retraced their steps to the village gate and rode back into the thick jungle.

Chapter 6

THE RUSTED STATION

'I think I may save my crocus thing for later too,' Daniel said, politely waiting until they were out of earshot of the Phibs.

The hills below the treeline diminished, and the floor of the great forest became flatter the farther they travelled. Just north of the village they came to a wide, fast-flowing river, over which a strong wooden bridge continued the path to the other side. As Alpona trotted across the bridge, Daniel leant over and looked down into the current. It wasn't too deep in places, and he could see some large stones below the surface.

'What's the name of this river?' he shouted, in order to be heard over the noise.

'The Dran,' Alpona bellowed.

Once across the bridge, they followed the track through the jungle known as the Savan Road, past great snaking tree-roots and thick bushes with emerald-green leaves.

After many hours of riding through the dark rainforest Daniel was feeling very tired, and closed his eyes.

Suddenly, a dart-like flash of light burst through the trees, and, blinded for an instant, Daniel turned his head away. After a few moments, he opened his eyes carefully and saw that he was still sitting on Alpona's back. He glanced back at Ketch, who was now wearing tinted goggles.

'Can't let the light bother you here,' Ketch said. 'I made these to protect my eyes from the sun in Iria and from sun-trap reflections. Fashioned some for her also ...'

Daniel turned back round and watched Alpona's head bobbing up and down as she galloped. He saw the edges of a pair of large sun goggles she was now wearing of the same design.

'We stopped, but didn't want to disturb you. I can make a pair for you too, later,' Ketch said.

'Thanks,' Daniel said. 'How close are we to this station?'

'It's not far to the edge of the forest,' Alpona said. 'A few hundred feet and we'll break cover. From there we'll be able to see the Rusted Station. Getting on a transporter for Jassk City is the plan. We need to keep in mind that Delvidran soldiers may be looking for you.'

'They are probably still after us from when the troops followed you into the jungle,' Ketch said. 'Their captain, whom I believe you've met ... she's, well, let's just say she doesn't give up easily.'

'She is in command of all of the king's forces,' Alpona explained. 'The Radiants only take orders from her and the king. You don't want to get in a tussle with one of them—those foul creatures use light energy against their enemies.'

'Light energy? Like the sun's rays?' Daniel asked.

'More like electricity,' Ketch said. 'Biotricity it's called.'

'*Bio*tricity?' Daniel said.

'Similar to lightning,' Alpona said. 'One bolt will make your skin bubble until your eyes pop out of your skull.'

Daniel did not want to imagine that right now.

'Here's the end of the trees,' Alpona said.

The light was almost unbearable now. Daniel held his hands over his face for a few seconds until his eyes adjusted.

'And there's the station,' said Alpona.

Between his fingers Daniel could make out a large red shape. Seconds later, he noticed a tall structure about a mile away in a valley that sloped gently away from them. He thought its massive swirls at one end looked like a hermit crab's shell. Except this shell was made from a rust-red material, similar to old iron. Running through the station from the west and out to the north was a shiny silver railway track, clearly better maintained than the building itself. A small rectangular shape in the distance sped along the tracks to the north of the station. Daniel could also make out the movement of people, little dots moving to and from the shell.

Alpona stopped to munch some grass.

'Come on, horsey!' Ketch said with a grin. 'Time's a-wasting.'

'Ketch, the train to Jassk leaves every half an hour,' Alpona said. 'Please let me eat in some semblance of peace. And desist from saying *horsey*.'

Ketch got off Alpona's back. A few feet away, with his

back against a tree, Ketch checked his three pistols.

'Is he always like this?' Daniel asked Alpona in a hushed tone.

'I don't go on adventures with him very often—we have very different leadership styles,' she replied with a sigh.

Daniel tried not to grin.

'We still have to get our tickets,' Ketch said, 'and the Rusted Station is slow at the best of times.'

Ketch joined Daniel once more on Alpona's back. Daniel's legs felt sore – a reminder of how long he had been riding. Alpona galloped slower than usual down the mild slope and across the plain, until the swirling tower of the station loomed above them.

'Do you know why the station has been left to rust?' Daniel asked. 'The track looks almost new.'

'Commerce,' Alpona said. 'Since Jassk and Delvidran negotiated an alliance a few years ago, traders from Iria have been banned from travelling to the city to buy or sell goods. It's all part of the Delvidran king's wish to squeeze the Irians until they submit to his rule. That's part of the reason why the Phibs are more interested in bartering.'

'That's terrible. The track through the stop is kept up to date whilst the station for Iria is left to age?'

'Exactly. For the sake of traders and passengers living farther down the line,' Ketch explained.

'Hmmm, the Irians should show the king that he can't

get away with things like that. The Phibs and talking horses and all the others in the jungle could get together against him.'

'That's all very well, but his Radiants have the advantage. Even the ministers of Jassk fear them,' Alpona said. 'The other Sacred, the "talking horses" as you call us, have migrated somewhere across the Broken Waste, beyond the king's reach, so even if all of the Phibs in Iria marched on Delvidran, their numbers would not be high enough to oppose his army.'

'So how did you stop the Delvidrans before?' Daniel asked, intrigued.

'Guerrilla tactics,' Ketch said. 'Attacking without being seen. But that is only useful if they are cut off from their supplies, and every time they flee into their castle the game starts all over again.'

'It's time to get the tickets,' Ketch said.

He and Daniel dismounted Alpona. Ketch put the hood of his jacket up, and then removed his sun goggles and Alpona's.

'Why have you put your hood up?' Daniel asked with concern.

He gave no reply, and strode towards the station entrance. As they approached, the glass doors automatically slid open.

Inside, they walked through a huge, dusty entrance hall,

where people were milling about. Some were walking towards the entrances to the platforms. Some were seated on chairs at the sides of the hallway. Some were standing checking monitors fixed to metal poles that hung from the ceiling displaying destinations and times. Some were buying tickets from machines and manned kiosks, and others were using the vending machines. These were the first machines Daniel had seen in this world that resembled the ones on Earth.

'The next train is in six minutes,' Ketch said.

'Ketch, could I borrow some money for a snack? I'm very hungry,' Daniel said.

'I would, but things are a bit different here,' Ketch explained.

He raised his right hand and pulled up the sleeve of his shirt. Daniel could see a barcode made of green light on his wrist and a digital display below it which read '000000701200' in green numbers.

'Here, each person's transactions are traced by the ruling class, and in case the king thinks I may be with you, we don't want that, so you'll have to wait until we get to my friend's place in Jassk for food ... I'm sorry. One of the ticketing staff who works here is another friend of mine. She'll give me free tickets. Alpona and I helped her family a while back.'

Ketch went over to the glass-fronted ticket booth, where a well-dressed young woman was sitting.

'What are those numbers Ketch has on his wrist? Does

he pay for stuff with them? One of the Delvidran soldiers in the castle had the exact same thing on his wrist,' Daniel said.

'The numbers are the amount of altins that Ketch has at the moment,' Alpona explained.

'Altins?'

'Altinor's currency. When he is paid for jobs, he receives altins to the digital currency storer embedded in his arm via an employer's or client's altin emitter, and the payment is added to his existing total. It's how all people are paid in our world, except those of the ruling class; at least that's what they call themselves.'

'Who are they?' said Daniel.

'The ruling class? They're the rulers and their families of each territory of Altinor. They see themselves as too important to carry digital currency storers embedded in their bodies.'

'Can you get me something from the machine, then? Please,' Daniel asked Alpona.

'I can't.'

'Why not? Have you run out of money?'

'I'm a horse.'

'Don't horses receive altins?'

'Free horses like me and the other Sacred have no need for such methods of control. And even if I had one and paid with it, it would be traced.'

'All done,' Ketch said, returning from the booth with a

smile on his face.

FZZZ. GOT 'EM. VOICE DETECTION CONFIRMED. BOOM.

The three of them barely had time to see what was happening, but they all leapt instinctively away from the noise.

A moment later, Daniel got up from the floor, shaken but uninjured. One of the vending machines to the left of where they had been standing was on fire, its glass smashed in. Ketch was on his feet, and Alpona was a few feet ahead of him, galloping towards something. She skidded on the stone floor, turned and gave an enormous kick of her hind legs. Daniel saw something large and made of metal land on the hallway floor; it bore a vague resemblance to a bird, a falcon or great hawk perhaps, with shiny black feathers.

'Searcher!' Alpona shouted. 'We have to get to the transporter, right now!'

The metal bird flew up and hurtled through the air towards them.

Ketch dashed along the corridor, grabbed Daniel's arm and pulled him towards the platform entrance.

'Searchers aren't friendly!' he shouted as they all ran.

'I gathered that!' Daniel said. 'It's platform one for Jassk.'

'Correct. Alpona, duck!'

The horse dropped at once to one side, bringing her legs down just in time. The Searcher flew over her like a dart, spraying small sparks that burned Alpona's flank, making her squeal in pain. People in the great metal bird's path were screaming and diving out of its way.

Ketch took a flintlock from his belt and with a click, cocked it and turned to face their pursuer. Daniel had almost forgotten that Ketch carried pistols.

BLAM!

In a flash of smoke and fire, he took the shot and the Searcher hit the floor, sparks flying from its dented head. Running through the entrance to platform one, Daniel leapt through the open doors of a train that hovered a foot above the track, soon followed by Ketch.

'Alpona, come on!' Ketch shouted.

Alpona was now on the platform, but the dented Searcher had managed to regain flight and was chasing her. From a hole in its right wing, the metal bird fired a bola at her galloping hooves; the interconnected weights made an eerie sound in flight. Daniel winced as they found their mark, tangling around Alpona's legs and making her fall feet from the train.

'LEAVING NOW FOR JASSK CITY. PLEASE HOLD ON,' said the train's robotic public address system.

'No!' Daniel shouted.

'Alpona!' Ketch shouted. 'Hold on, I'm coming!'

But before he could leave the carriage, the thick metal doors shut in front of him.

'Damn!' Ketch shouted.

He wrestled with the handle, trying to force the door open.

'Can't you open it?' Daniel said, panicking.

'Once they shut, they don't open till the next stop. We've got to think of something!'

In a few seconds the train's engines fired up. Hovering above the railway, with lightning bolts of electricity crackling between the train and the tracks, it began to move out of the crab shell station. Once clear of the platform, it accelerated rapidly. Out of the carriage window Daniel could see Alpona crouched forward, her back legs tangled in the bola cord, thrashing her head from side to side, squealing in pain and frustration. Delvidran soldiers were now on the platform, spears aimed at her side. They cut the bola cord and forced her to stand, while the captain Daniel had the misfortune of meeting before inspected the grounded metal bird.

It was too painful to watch, and he pulled his head away from the window.

'Where's the next stop? We need to help her!' Daniel said, his throat dry.

'Jassk,' Ketch said. 'They'll interrogate her.'

'We'll get the next train back, follow them from there.'

'By then they'll be halfway to Delvidran.'

They were both silent for a moment. Daniel looked around at the other passengers, most of whom looked bored or tired, seemingly unaware of what had just happened.

'We'll have to proceed with our plan to find the second part of the stardeath generator,' Ketch said.

'But Alpona will be stuck in the castle, injured and most likely scared, with no one to help her!'

'You think I don't know that?' Ketch snarled. 'If we return to the Rusted Station, they'll reach Delvidran long before we can catch up with them. It's virtually impossible to get into Mornaren Castle unnoticed. Believe me, I've tried.'

'I'm smaller ... maybe I could try,' Daniel suggested.

'No, that's too risky. They can torture her for information ... but they won't kill her. They'll use her as bait. The captain will hope you return to try to save her, then they'll pounce. I know she would want us to carry on. We'll look for the jewel in the city and think of a way to free her. The Jasskians have an alliance with the king, but—'

'I know,' Daniel interrupted, 'Alpona mentioned it.'

'The Jasskians fear the king's Radiants and his wish to expand into others' territory. We'll think of a way ...'

Daniel slumped back in his seat and Ketch sat down next to him. *Surely there was more they could do?* This king appeared to have everyone on Altinor worried or frightened. Daniel peered through the carriage window. The train shot past the landscape at an incredible pace, the plains either side of the track whirring past in a blur of yellow and green against the dimming light of the sun in a vast cloudless sky. It would soon be evening and they would be in Jassk. Another new place. Home felt further away than ever.

Chapter 7

JASSK

Daniel could see a woman surrounded by darkness. As he approached, he realised it was his mum.

'Daniel! My sweet boy! Where have you been?' she cried, running to him with her arms wide open to hug him.

But to Daniel's horror, she did not stop and passed right through him.

'Mum! Mum! Why can't you hold me?'

He woke with a sharp jolt. The train had stopped alongside a platform.

'We're here,' Ketch told him.

Out of the window a vast dome could be seen above the station. Putting his nose against the glass, Daniel looked up at the bright stars through the dome roof. Thousands ... Millions. They seemed so close. He wondered if any might be Earth.

With a loud whoosh, the carriage doors of the hover-train opened. Even though it was night-time, the air that entered felt comfortable and warm.

They exited the train and walked down the platform.

'We're going to see if Gressil's in his shop. Then we'll stay at my friend's place,' Ketch said.

'Gressil?'

'The merchant.'

They passed several monitors set side by side on the station wall. One read *New flats in Zero-C Dome*, and showed the layout of an example home rotating in holographic 3D. It was a far cry from the Rusted Station.

'We have this on Earth,' Daniel said; 'I just haven't seen it on an advert before.'

'You don't have this, though,' Ketch said.

Daniel looked at another screen showing colourful adverts for energy, with what seemed to be tall radio masts forming a wheel-like shape through a city dome. The image, also in 3D, changed to show a home, then a car and finally, a man talking on a mobile phone. The script read: 'Subscribe to your own clean, unlimited supply of energy for any electrical requirement, be it your home, your vehicle or your phone – power up with City Surge. You pay just 200 altins per calendar month, and with your device's *install beams*, you can take what you need from the grid and away you go. City Surge – your energy, for a brighter tomorrow.'

Daniel was astonished.

'So they get electricity from the air?'

'Yes,' Ketch said. 'Electricity is pumped through radio waves to everyone who pays for the connection.'

'Whoa! That means you would never need phone adapters or ... or petrol for cars!'

'Ah, well, the waves alone don't make the cars run here. The Jasskians also use a form of fuel.'

'What's that?'

'Jasskian waste.'

'What, like recycling?'

'No, human waste.'

'*Human waste*?!'

'Not the way you know it,' Ketch said, with no hint of a smile. 'After the city's sewage system separates the excretions from other waste, it processes it in tanks with chemicals to remove the smell and texture, and converts it into a purchasable biofuel. Animal waste, too.'

'Disgusting ... but brilliant,' Daniel said with a look of amazement on his face.

They turned a corner and headed out to the city under a great central dome that looked several thousand feet high. Stopping in front of a row of strange pod-like vehicles, they watched as people got into them before being shot along various tracks running through the air.

'Let's see if we can reach the market.'

Two people got out of the nearest pod. The pod door opened upwards, like on the cockpits he had seen on fighter planes in films. Ketch and Daniel got in it and the pod doors soon closed automatically. Taking their seats, Daniel noticed what looked like a camera lens within the pod's dashboard pointed at them.

Ketch pressed a button next to a display bearing the words 'Central Market' on the pod's dashboard.

'BZZT. DESTINATION: CENTRAL MARKET. PLEASE HOLD ON.'

Suddenly, the pod shot across the tracks like a ball being fired from a cannon.

'It's free?' Daniel shouted above the whoosh of the pod.

'Yep. Paid for with public money. They have very high taxes here,' Ketch said.

Less than a minute later, with Daniel's cheeks feeling like they had retreated to the back of his head, the transport-pod ground to a halt with a crackle of brakes. The pod door opened.

He unclipped his seat's safety straps and stepped out onto the platform at the entrance to the market. Ketch followed. Ahead of Daniel was a daze of hustle and bustle, movement and colour. With a loud crackle of electricity the pod they had used sped off along the track.

'I ... can't feel my teeth,' Daniel said.

Ketch smiled. 'Surely you've been on a roller coaster on Earth?'

Much to Daniel's annoyance, he had not been allowed on a decent roller-coaster ride yet as he was still too short. He had begged his mum to take him and his sister to a theme park and remembered one of the rides from the brochure called The Embalmer. What he had just experienced made him question the sanity of his wish.

This place was distracting them from helping Alpona. Ketch started to walk towards the market and Daniel followed a few steps behind.

'Where is the person you traded the machine part with? We have to get it quickly and rescue Alpona,' Daniel said.

'His shop is just a few minutes' walk up here, to the left.'

'Great! So we can get the machine part today?'

'Well yes, if he hasn't sold it. We can't be sure of anything. Let's just hope the shop's still open and he's there.'

Daniel hadn't even considered the trader might have sold the jewel. Getting the belt from Phorm at the Phib village had been hair-raising enough, and the thought of them chasing a trader on some old information worried him. He resolved to stay positive. Things always seemed easier that way. His mum said by being positive you attract good things to your life.

Ketch's confident strides past a melee of merchants, shoppers and what looked like robot containers speeding through the streets proved difficult to keep up with. To make it easier, Daniel tried to emulate his exact path through the throng. He brushed against dividing walls that jutted out between stalls and shops, and bumping into, but not upsetting, tables of various wares. The number of different things for sale was vast. He saw fresh fish laid out on several stalls, some with *more than two eyes*, which made Daniel stop and look. More stalls displayed large weird-looking blue vegetables shaped like fern leaves. On others were metal cases which Daniel imagined to be batteries of differing sizes. Suddenly, Ketch turned left down a smaller street lined with stalls of gleaming rocks and precious stones. Now they were getting somewhere. Remaining on the pavement throughout Rare Street, however, proved unachievable.

Seeing a gap in the market's traffic, Daniel broke into a light jog up the centre of the street to see which shop Ketch was going to stop at. In order to dodge a large dog running after another straight past him, he ended up stepping in a great muddy puddle by the kerbside.

'Arggh! That's all I need.'

He began to think of Alpona, and imagined her walking across the plains, being dragged along by the captain, her troops and that twisted metal hawk. Then he thought of his mum and Rachel. Muddy and tired, his eyes welled up.

Ketch, who had been looking back every so often to make sure he was keeping up, stopped and walked back to him.

'Are you all right?' he asked in a low voice. 'You're thinking about Alpona, aren't you?'

Daniel turned his face away and wiped his tears with the hem of his T-shirt.

'I'm fine,' he said.

'Come on, let's check the shop and then we can rest and plan what we can do to help Alpona.'

Daniel was glad Ketch changed the subject. He was right, there was nothing they could do at the moment. The journey to see home again was important, but Alpona's life was their priority.

Daniel straightened up, shoulders back.

'If the trader doesn't have it, then we must go back for Alpona tomorrow,' Daniel said. He didn't try to hide his exhaustion.

'I'm sorry I've not stopped,' Ketch apologised. 'Truth is, the Jasskian consul and his government don't hold me in high regard after my last visit.'

Daniel was cheered by this news.

'First the Delvidrans, then the Phibs and Jassk—is there anyone you haven't managed to annoy?' he joked.

They both chuckled.

'Only one person, my wife, but she treated me badly in a completely different way.'

'How's that?'

'Never wanted to have apple crumble after dinner.'

Daniel smiled. 'You have apple crumble here?'

'Yes! What do you think we are, savages?' Ketch smiled.

Daniel didn't have to wait long to find out if the shop was still open. Continuing down Rare Street, he saw a large, bold red sign above a doorway that read 'Gressil's'. Ketch strode up to the sturdy-looking door and pressed the small bell.

After a few seconds, a low gargling voice came through a speaker by the door.

'Speak! We're closing in a few moments.'

'Gressil. It's Ketch,' Ketch said in a low voice. 'I'm with a friend. We're here to discuss a trade.'

'Ketch! I might be able to spare a moment. I hope you have something good for me. Come up!'

'What's this Gressil like?' Daniel asked, the buzz of a door-entry system clamouring in the background.

Ketch pushed open the metal door.

'You'll soon find out.'

A huge set of stairs led up to a glass door, through which Daniel could see an elderly, skeletal man approaching along a corridor. The man opened the door to greet them.

'Hello, Ketch. The timing is ill-chosen, given your current reputation with the Council, but I'm always prepared to hear a trade if it's of some worth.'

'Gressil, thank you for seeing us at this late hour. This is my friend, Daniel.'

'Pleased to meet you, Daniel. Do you also live in Iria?'

Daniel, unsure what to say, considered lying, but he felt certain this would do more harm than good.

'I don't. I am from—'

'He's from abroad,' Ketch interrupted.

'Abroad? Past the Broken Waste, somewhere like that?' Gressil smiled. 'Well, please sit down.'

He beckoned them towards two ornate armchairs by a dark wooden writing desk. Behind the desk was an even fancier armchair. The design of the chairs and many other things in the room seemed strangely familiar to Daniel. He and Ketch sat in the armchairs. Maps of various lands were framed on the wall between high glass cases storing a variety of goods. He recognised an old vacuum cleaner with the letters O–O-V-E-R on its plastic body, the H at the start scuffed off with age. *How on Earth did Gressil get hold of that?*

'Mera!' Gressil shouted down an ancient microphone system on his desk.

A light-haired young woman emerged from a small wooden swing door to one side of the desk. She looked unhappy.

'Please get these gentlemen what they wish to drink. Ketch, Jasskian strong-ale? A Forjan firewater?'

'I'll just have a glass of glacier water, thank you, Mera,' Ketch replied.

'Daniel, what would you like?' Gressil asked.

Daniel was going to ask for the same as Ketch due to his lack of knowledge of the fineries of Altinorean refreshment, but a memory led him to request something else.

'Hot chocolate, please.'

Gressil and Mera looked at each other, then at Ketch, who smiled and shrugged.

'Er, I do not believe that we have this ... *hot chocopat?*'

Gressil said. 'A whistberry sherb, would that do?'

'I think you might like it,' Ketch said, smiling.

'Okay, thanks. I'll try that,' Daniel agreed.

'My usual,' Gressil said, looking at Mera.

The young woman nodded to Gressil with an air of resignation and left through the swing door.

'Well then, Ketch, let's hear what trade you have in mind.'

As Ketch began to speak, Mera came back and placed each drink in front of them on the table. Daniel's was green and fizzy. Ketch's glacier water looked like water on Earth. Gressil's drink, standing on a glass coaster on his desk, was blue. Daniel thought it looked like mouthwash.

'This rare sun-trap,' Ketch said, taking it from his jacket pocket, 'in exchange for the green jewel I traded you for korcite a while ago. If you still have it, that is.'

Gressil's and Daniel's eyes narrowed upon viewing the object Ketch had placed on the merchant's desk. Ketch pressed a button on the side of the metal cylinder, and the sun-trap opened with a click to form a small dish for collecting energy.

'May I?' Gressil asked.

'Please,' Ketch agreed.

Gressil inspected the sun-trap, turning it carefully in his hands. Daniel noticed a barcode and currency display on his wrist. The rivers of blue veins around his currency storer looked like they were about to pop out. The frail merchant left the sun-trap on his desk.

'Sun-traps are indeed hard to come by in Jassk,' Gressil said, 'but I do not know off the top of my head to whom I might sell it. Besides, it is not worth as much as the jewel.'

'Do you still have the jewel?' Ketch said.

Daniel was distracted for a moment by his whistberry sherb. Seconds after swallowing a mouthful of the green liquid, his eyes bulged and his nostrils flared—it was like a lemon had exploded on contact with his stomach, and this sensation seared back up through his gullet into his mouth.

'Cough, cough!' Daniel was trying not to show his discomfort too much. Behind clenched teeth, his tongue attempted to fan his mouth back to its normal state.

'Something the matter, Daniel? Mera!' Gressil shouted through the microphone. 'Please fetch the young gentleman a zaffer clarsact.'

'She'll make you one of these,' Gressil smiled, pointing to his blue drink.

'No! No, please, it's okay, I'm okay, thank you.'

'Hold the clarsact,' Gressil spoke through the microphone, dismayed.

Ketch smiled. 'The boy's not used to sherbs,' he said lightly. 'Shall we get back to the subject?'

Daniel ground his teeth but tried to keep his face neutral and not draw too much attention to himself.

'I haven't got the jewel you traded here last year,' Gressil said. 'Things change hands quickly here—green and red stones are currently in great demand in the city.'

He looked through his desk drawers and produced a ledger.

'What I can give you is the name of the vendor who bought it, and their position.'

'Position?' Daniel said.

Gressil opened the ledger and searched through its pages.

'Ah yes, one of the consul's own merchants. Came in about a year ago, not long after you traded it. Took a great interest in the stones I had. Bought the thing for a packet, registered—yes—registered in the paperwork that they were buying on behalf of the palace.'

'The consul ... well, that makes things trickier. Thank you for the drinks, Gressil, and the information,' Ketch said.

Daniel could tell Ketch wanted to leave swiftly. Ketch stood up from his chair and hinted to Daniel to do the same.

'Wait, Woodsman. I appreciate the deal you have brought to me, but I've thought of one you must hear.'

The trader opened the bottom drawer and produced a gun just like Ketch's, with a metal ring on the bottom of its grip for storing it. Gressil cocked and aimed it at Ketch. Ketch moved a hand down towards the pistol clipped to his belt.

'Primed,' Gressil said. 'Don't think of matching. While you've been away the consul thought it best to put a price on your head. It's not personal.'

'How much are they offering?' Ketch asked.

Daniel felt his heart pounding. The gun was trained on Ketch, but there was a slim chance Daniel could reach Gressil before he changed his aim.

'That would be telling, and I don't want to embarrass you.'

'Well, you'd better keep your arm steady if you want to collect.'

Gressil snorted. 'Oh, I will,' he said. 'In fact ... Mera? Call the City Watch and inform them that if they wish to secure the capture of one of their "Most Wanted", the Delvidran, Ketch Raynott, then they had better get to Gressil's right now.'

In that moment, each second felt like an eternity. Daniel launched himself from the armchair towards Gressil, and the trader's flintlock fired as they fell back over the desk chair.

There was now a large bullet hole in the back wall behind Ketch's armchair. Daniel and Gressil rolled around, locked in a struggle for the weapon. Daniel gripped Gressil's arm firmly, causing him to lift the hand that was clasping the pistol towards the ceiling. After a few seconds the aged man gave in, releasing the gun. Daniel kicked the gun away from his hand to make sure, but Gressil's chance had gone when the shot was fired.

'Leave him, Daniel, he's not worth spit. We have to get

out of here before the City Watch arrive,' Ketch said, picking up Gressil's gun.

THUMP. THUMP. THUMP.

The door at the bottom of the stairs rattled with deafening knocks.

'GRESSIL! THIS IS THE CITY WATCH!'

'You were saying?' Daniel said.

'There's another way out via a door in the kitchen,' Mera said. 'The stairs from the kitchen lead to a backstreet.'

Ketch thanked her while picking up Gressil's gun.

THUMP. THUMP. THUMP.

'GRESSIL, OPEN THIS DOOR!'

'You won't get far, Ketch. Jassk is a hard city to hide in,' Gressil croaked.

'So long, Gressil,' said Ketch. He grabbed the sun-trap back off the merchant's desk.

Ketch and Daniel ran out the room and met Mera in the corridor.

'There's another way out,' she smiled, 'second door on the left. The stairs through it lead to a backstreet.'

They thanked her, dashed through the door, pounded down the stairs and ran out of the shop.

Night filled the domes of the city, broken only by the many lights from the buildings and illuminated neon signs. Having escaped the City Watch, Ketch took Daniel to a hotel in a quiet side street of Market Dome, where a large white sign swinging above the entrance bore the name *Yavos* in blue letters.

'This place is owned by friends of mine. They'll give us a room and some food,' he said.

Daniel doubted they could stay here for too long with soldiers searching the city for them.

Ketch gave the black-haired woman at the hotel reception a hug. She was called Niya. They chatted for a while, and then she showed them to a room. It was small, but cosy, and had a tiny en suite. The view looked across tiled rooftops beneath the enormous dome that enclosed the city's markets. The buildings here were crumbling and only a few floors high, unlike the shiny skyscrapers within the larger dome that could be seen in the distance, stretching high amongst the clouds, all within their own self-contained world.

Daniel chose a bed and lay down in exhaustion. He wanted to sleep, but his stomach rumbled loudly and he realized how hungry he was.

'I'll see if I can get us some food from Niya. Can't risk going out again. Back in a tick,' Ketch said.

After several attempts at drifting off, Daniel got up and used the loo. To his surprise, it was very much like the ones in his own world. When he had washed his hands and face in the sink, he looked up and saw his reflection in the mirror. He felt older. He grabbed a towel, rubbed his face dry and went back into the room.

Ketch's return was marked by a click of the door and two large foil-wrapped plates. Under the see-through plastic were two layered shapes, each layer a different colour. They did not look like food; more that someone had squashed rainbows into tiny squares.

'You've got to try this.' Ketch grinned.

'Niya gave you those? What are they?' Daniel sat up on the bed.

'Them, and these,' Ketch said, throwing two plastic bottles containing red juice onto his own bed. 'Just try the food.'

While Daniel scrambled for one of the bottles, Ketch put a plate on the wooden desk with some cutlery and took his own multi-coloured square to eat on his bed. Daniel had a swig of the dark red juice, which tasted far tamer than the drink at Gressil's shop. It was similar to fresh raspberry juice though a little more sour.

He got up and took the foil off his plate. He didn't think the cake-like square was going to taste nice, let alone fill him up, but his hunger led him to try a piece. Carving a slice off the square with a metal implement similar to a fork but with six prongs, he brought it to his mouth. The slice had only touched his tongue when Daniel's taste buds were sent spinning with flavour. In that moment, the square – red, yellow, green, blue, purple, indigo, orange – connected with his brain in an explosion of memory.

'Thanks, this is incredible, Ketch! I've been so hungry since we left the train station. What is it? Tastes like turkey, roast potatoes, green beans and cranberry sauce, all in one!'

'No problem. I said I'd get you fed. Later rather than sooner unfortunately, but there you go. It's plant-based with some natural seasoning. Like your soya. You saved me back there, Daniel. I owe you a massive thank you.'

'Don't mention it. I knew there was something strange about Gressil,' Daniel said between mouthfuls. The small "rainbow square", as he named it, turned out to be deceptively filling.

'I want you to have this,' Ketch said, and unclipped a flintlock from his belt. 'I know Gressil didn't deserve having one of my pistols. Officially, Jasskians aren't permitted to have guns. The city's Council banned them, though I wouldn't be surprised if someone is making one or two unofficially. Jasskian and Delvidran cultures share one thing in common: they don't like using guns. They have always seen them as cowardly weapons. I personally don't share their scruples.'

'It's strange the Delvidrans see using guns as cowardly, but use those Radiant things to shoot lightning.'

Ketch laughed. 'I traded the gun with Gressil for some jewels I could use in my machines,' he continued. 'Come on, take it!'

He passed the gun to Daniel. Daniel swallowed the last mouthful of his rainbow square. He was full.

'Are you sure?'

'You remember how to load it?'

Daniel nodded. He placed his empty plate on the table in the room.

'Here's some normal powder, primer powder and ammunition,' Ketch said, handing Daniel a pouch of bullets and pouring out some powder and primer into two unused flasks.

'I'm very grateful, but I'm not certain I'll be able to use it,' Daniel said, feeling the weight of the gun.

'Of course you will! But, understand, it should *only* be used in self-defence,' Ketch said, passing him a metal measure, a wadding pouch, a bag of flints and the now full powder flasks.

Daniel fixed everything to his belt using the rings attached to each. He wondered how Ketch was able to run with all this weight hanging from him.

'Remember to point it down at all times when you don't intend to use it. Always keep it primed, in good condition and do not lose it. You never know when you might need it.'

He slumped back onto his bed, still wearing his boots, and after a few moments fell into a snore-filled sleep. Daniel decided to do one more thing before sleeping, and went through the weapon drill Ketch had demonstrated. Once he had been successful in remembering each stage, feeling tired but content, he pushed a bullet down the barrel using the ramrod, left the pistol uncocked on the bedside table and closed his eyes.

Chapter 8

SELF-DEFENCE

The next morning, harsh streaks of sunlight poured through the gap in the curtains. Ketch and Daniel washed in the shower in the tiny en suite bathroom and ate some tasty waffle-like pastries from Niya. The plan was to get a train from Jassk's main railway station to the Rusted Station before finding transport to Delvidran, perhaps a horse-drawn cart or some similar vehicle they could conceal themselves in, and a willing driver. It would be a step further away from getting the jewel and going home, but Alpona was a prisoner and somehow they had to find a way into Delvidran Castle and free her. As for the jewel, it had apparently been bought on behalf of the consul, and it would take some time to work out how to get into the consul's palace and get it back.

'Come on, time to go,' Ketch said.

Daniel picked up the gun from the bedside table. He checked it was uncocked and slid it between his trousers and stomach, making sure the curved handle of the flintlock was concealed beneath his T-shirt.

A crowd of people passed by as they walked along the main thoroughfare of Market Dome.

'Do the Jasskians like the Delvidran king?' Daniel said in

a low voice.

'Jassk is advanced and the largest city we know of on Altinor. Regardless of what its government might want, many of its inhabitants are traders and most do not wish the city to use its power against other peoples and lands, for it would disrupt trade. The alliance Jassk and Delvidran share is unfortunate—a marriage of convenience. The Jasskian consul and government don't believe they could withstand an attack from Delvidran.'

'You're talking like Alpona,' Daniel said, laughing.

'Am I? Ha, well, I suppose she would say something like that.' Ketch smiled.

'Jassk couldn't withstand an attack from Delvidran because of the king's machines?'

Ketch nodded. 'The Radiants. The agreement suits Jassk because they believe it gives them time to create an effective means of resisting such weapons. Many think they are doing this in secret, as nothing has been mentioned officially.'

They passed the fish stalls Daniel had seen and smelt on their way to Gressil's. One woman was pressing buttons on a handheld device before attaching it to a stove in front of her. The stove ignited in a violent flash of yellow flame.

Daniel inhaled sharply.

'What ... what happened?' he asked, pointing at the stove, which now had fish frying on its top.

'City Surge. Energy straight off the grid,' Ketch

explained.

They continued towards the transport-pod platform.

'What did you do to anger the government, Ketch?'

Ketch stopped and turned.

'Shhhh! Can't say here. Wait till we reach the platform where there will be less people around.'

Daniel bit his lip and felt foolish for forgetting they were still fugitives from the City Watch. He could wait for an answer.

After a few minutes they were at the transport-pod platform. Instead of joining the rather long queue for pods, Ketch moved to the quieter side of the platform. He looked one way, then the other in a shifty manner.

'I am on the Council's "Most Wanted" list because of something I sold last year. A primary construct,' Ketch said.

'The same time you traded the jewel? Primary construct, what's that?' Daniel said.

Ketch looked around again. No one was in earshot.

'It's a type of machine, like what you call a robot.'

'What was wrong with that?'

'The robot can be programmed to make all sorts of things, from pots and pans to engines and circuitry,' Ketch said. 'The consul found out that the train carriage manufacturer I sold it to had travelled to the castle and sold it to the captain, breaking one of the key terms of Jassk's alliance with Delvidran. Remember those Searcher things?

The captain's been using it to make those and who knows what else. While you were in the castle did you notice if she has progressed as far as electrification of it?'

'The only light in the castle was sunlight when I was there, and they had unlit candles on stands,' Daniel said.

'She hasn't worked out how ... yet. Due to the alliance between Delvidran and Jassk, instead of blaming Delvidran and the merchant, Jassk are blaming the original seller, *me*.'

'I can't believe it.'

'The man I sold it to was arrested. He's probably lying in a city jail cell. Or he might have been executed.'

Daniel looked down at the metallic floor of the platform and then up again.

'The Delvidrans don't use guns, right? Same as the people here. The king surely won't allow her to use the robot to make them.'

'I wouldn't put much faith in the king upholding any cultural values or traditions. I programmed the construct to activate only after the input of a set of passcodes, so it would not be used by anyone without my permission. I programmed it not to have any blueprints in its memory that it could access to make guns or projectile weapons—but the bola thrower on that Searcher broke the rules. The captain found someone who has cracked the codes and reprogrammed the primary construct. The captain may now be trying to create other useful tech for the army, including things I refused to make for the king. Gressil, the backstabber that he is, kept his word never to sell the flintlock he bought from me. Makes me wish I'd never made those things.'

'Let's get to Delvidran,' Daniel said, moving towards the queue.

'A few months earlier,' Ketch continued, 'I was informed by traders in Ao Sirt that the penalty for me setting foot inside Jassk again would be capture and execution.'

It was their turn to enter a transport-pod, and Ketch selected the destination.

'BZZT. DESTINATION: STATION DOME. PLEASE HOLD ON.'

Daniel realised that many of the things Ketch said he had spent his life working on had been used against him. Gressil's flintlock pistol was just one example.

'Try not to act like you are not from here,' Ketch said to Daniel.

'What are we doing waiting here?' Daniel asked when they'd stopped near the entrance to Jassk's main railway station.

'Quiet, please,' Ketch said. 'We have to talk to the guards and see if they'll let us pass.'

A guard at the entrance asked for identification and the purpose for their travel. Ketch had continued to wear his jacket hood up throughout the city to avoid recognition, though Daniel thought this probably attracted *more* attention.

'So no documents ... names?' the squat, dull-eyed soldier asked.

He was brandishing a spear not unlike the one the Delvidran captain carried.

'Alcaeon, and this is my nephew, Danieon.'

Daniel eyed Ketch but turned to the guard and smiled.

'We're—'

'Remove your hood,' the soldier ordered.

'Oh, excuse me,' Ketch feigned ignorance, pushing his hood back. 'As I was saying, we're travelling to Ao Sirt to return to my brother's house. We came for the market.'

'Buying or selling?'

'Selling, sir,' Daniel added.

'Now, Danieon, please let me talk to the lieutenant. Lieutenant, isn't it?'

'You are correct.'

'Lieutenant ...?'

'Lieutenant Baskin.'

'Now, Lieutenant Baskin,' Ketch continued, 'we are hoping to reach our village for dinner. We have forgotten our documents and for that I am sorry, but you can imagine going home to your wife ...'

'I haven't got a wife.'

'Do you have any pets?'

'A dog.'

'What's his name?'

'Carbine.'

'Right. You can imagine going home to Carbine at the end of your shift, both having a great dinner and afterwards putting your feet up and watching some monitorvisor.'

Daniel guessed this might be a television, but he was not altogether sure.

'Now, we don't have a dog,' Ketch continued, 'but we have a very similar vision—can you see it?'

Ketch put his arm around the guard's shoulder in an artful gesture.

'Yes, yes, I see,' the guard said, shrugging him off.

'Well, if you would allow us to catch the next train home, we'd be so grateful and think of you and Carbine when we are having food with Danieon's mum and dad. Ain't that right, Danieon?'

Daniel was beginning to get annoyed, but this was his cue.

'For sure, Uncle. I can't wait to show them some of these roasted crocus shoots I have.'

Ketch gave him a stern look.

'Wait a minute,' the guard said. 'I thought you were here selling.'

Ketch's face froze.

'Yeah, we traded whistberries for them,' Daniel said. 'Sometimes we can't get the sales so we barter, you know how it is.'

'Well no, I don't. To my knowledge, crocuses only grow in Iria. And only Phibs are permitted to sell them, and not in Jassk. You must have traded with a frog outside the city.'

'Yes, that's right, lieutenant,' Daniel said. 'He was a tall fellow.'

'And you say you made this exchange today?'

'That's right.'

'Thank you for that information. Guards!' the soldier shouted. 'Guards! Arrest these men!'

Before they could run, four guards patrolling the station a few feet away converged from each side, their spears held up in the air.

'Wait! Why are you arresting us?' Ketch asked.

'You can't have traded with a Phib,' the soldier said. 'According to Council reports, the Delvidrans wiped out Phibia, the last frog village, yesterday.'

Ketch was shocked and speechless. Daniel looked down at the criss-cross design of the station floor. He thought of the Phibs he had met in Iria, the scene of his first battle, and the generosity of the village towards them after his victory. He lashed out at the lieutenant, who was trying to grab hold of him, all the while cursing the fact that he had talked about the crocuses.

The rest of the guards were a few steps away from them, and in seconds they would be taken. Once they found out

118

who Ketch was, they would put him in jail, or worse. And Daniel would be seen as an accomplice. He wrenched the loaded pistol from his belt, primed and cocked it while the lieutenant advanced, stretched out his arm and fired just above the heads of the approaching guards.

BLAMMM.

'What are you doing?!' Ketch shouted.

The noise of the flintlock igniting and firing its shot surprised everyone. The guard checked his helmet.

'Come on!' Daniel shouted, running back towards the transport-pods.

Ketch turned and aimed at a spot above the oncoming guards.

BLAMMM.

The shot caused the soldiers to stop for a moment, only pursuing once they were sure no one had been hit. With his flintlock empty and the guards bearing down on them, Ketch turned to face the soldiers and slid forwards on his knees between the first two pursuers, stretching his arms out to connect his fists with their stomachs. The guard and Lieutenant Baskin fell either side of him, winded. Hearing sharp groans as knuckles met guts, Daniel turned round. Ketch got up and grabbed the two guards' spears, tossing one to Daniel.

'Don't look surprised. I was once in the army of the king.'

'I'm guessing they didn't teach you how to stop a bullet,' said a voice behind him.

Ketch turned. A guard had a flintlock trained on his mid-section.

BLAMMM.

Dropping his spear, Ketch fell first to his knees, then forwards onto the cold stone floor.

'Ketch!' Daniel shouted.

He ran over and crouched down. Ketch was motionless.

'I wouldn't come any closer if I were you,' the shooter warned.

Daniel froze. Where did the guard get that pistol if the Jasskians did not make weapons?

'Drop the spear,' said the guard with the gun.

Daniel released it and heard it ring on the stone floor.

'Why did you have to shoot him?' he shouted.

'He had a spear in his hand,' the guard said. 'He was bent on killing those guards.'

'That's not true! It was in self-defence! I'm going to see if he's okay,' Daniel said, moving forwards.

'What did I say, boy? Not a step closer,' the guard ordered.

The guard flipped Ketch's body over, and Daniel could see the almost black blood staining his shirt. His eyes became glassy.

'You've killed him! No, no, no!'

Daniel jumped on the guard's back, punching him repeatedly. Another guard bearing more pips on his shoulder arrived.

'Guard, take this body away! I don't want you creating any more of a scene in my railway station than this imbecile,' he growled, glaring at the soldier who shot Ketch.

The two guards obeyed their commander's order and dragged Ketch's body through a nearby doorway, over which hung a sign that read: *Cleaning Robots: Authorised Personnel Only.*

Daniel through his tears wanted to run, but the commander leaned down and grabbed his shoulder like a vice.

'We will need to question you about what has just occurred. Forward!'

The Jasskian soldier pushed Daniel ahead of him. Daniel, turning round, glared at the soldier. He did not know what to say, what lies to use or truth to tell. The soldier urged him on through a door near the station entrance using the butt of his spear. The sign read: *Soldiers' Quarters. Restricted.*

Daniel's heart was racing. What would happen to him if he told the truth? Would they believe he was from another world? Ketch was dead because of him! He didn't have to help him try to get home, but had done so anyway. Ketch would never see his wife again, thanks to him! He decided to tell the truth.

The guard pushed him onto a chair. He looked around the small grey office and across the desk cluttered with papers and unwashed mugs.

'Don't move!' the soldier commanded. 'Stay in that chair and answer my questions, or I will take you to the city courts and have you charged with assisting a criminal.'

'He isn't a criminal!' Daniel shouted. 'Why did you have to kill him?'

'My men were simply carrying out their duty. The man you say was your uncle resisted questioning and put up a struggle, so the guard shot him in self-defence. You will do well to remember that. Now, what were you doing in the city?'

'Liar!' Daniel shouted. 'He was shot because he was trying to help me. Why does your soldier have a gun? I thought Jasskians outlawed them!'

'This isn't a forum for debate,' the soldier said. '*You* are answering the questions, not me!'

The soldier walked round him and settled his spear on the back of the chair. Daniel jumped as he felt its point prodding his spine.

'Now tell me why you are here, and who you are,' the soldier said, 'or you won't live to see the courts.'

Daniel adjusted the rubber belt across his shoulder.

'My name is Daniel Mearns!' Daniel he, tears drying on his cheek. 'I am from another world and trying to get home.

The man your stupid soldier murdered wasn't my uncle. His name was Ketch. He was trying to help me get home. And you killed him!'

'My men informed me that you are both liars. You also resisted arrest. Lucky for you you were not killed too. Another world? Enough of the lies! What is your real motive for coming to our city? You are messengers for the Anti-Consul Movement, are you not?'

'No, I have never heard of the Anti-Consul ... whatever. I didn't even know the city had a consul until—'

The soldier slammed the wooden spear down on the back of the chair, grazing Daniel's back.

'You cannot play me, boy. No one your age under Altinor's sun has not heard of Jassk's consul.'

'Wait,' Daniel said, his wound starting to bleed, staining his shirt.

He gestured to the underside of his forearms.

'Look! There are no barcodes or displays. I am not from here. I'm telling the truth!'

The commander looked at his arms.

'You could have had yours removed. It has happened before. If you won't answer my questions, I won't detain you for trial. It will mean much less paperwork if I kill you. I can still get the truth out of you the fun way beforehand.'

The soldier took his spear from the back of the chair and walked round to face Daniel. Daniel leapt up and ran towards

123

him and the door beyond, but his efforts were in vain. The soldier pushed him back onto the chair and stuck his spear into Daniel's chest to one side of the rubber belt.

As Daniel screamed in agony and put up his hands to try to remove the spear, the commander twisted the point. It felt as though it was scraping a rib bone, the force of it pushing onto his lungs. It was hard to breathe.

With blood trickling out of him, Daniel remembered the flintlock hidden underneath his T-shirt that the guards had failed to see. He moved his trembling hand and clasped the butt of the pistol. Unable to load a bullet down the barrel, he took it out and threw it as hard as he could with what little strength he had left. It hit the soldier hard on the chest, causing him to let go of the spear. Daniel grabbed it and withdrew its point from his chest. He turned the spear round as the guard picked up the flintlock, aiming it at his head. The flintlock's hammer moved to strike the pan, but did not fire, as there was no bullet in the barrel. Daniel thrust the spear into the man's throat, pushing as hard as he could until the soldier fell to the floor. Letting go of the spear, Daniel collapsed.

Chapter 9

YAVOS HOTEL

Feeling excruciating pain, Daniel looked across the office at the soldier's body on the floor. Clutching the wound on his chest, which was still bleeding, he drew himself up by holding the chair so that he was sitting with his legs stretched out in front of him. *Is one of my ribs broken? What should I do now? Think, think.* He was surprised that no one had come into the guards' quarters. Assuming this office was where the soldiers should be when they weren't patrolling the station, he thought there must be a medical kit somewhere. With one hand against his chest, he searched the desk drawers, but there was nothing but papers and magazines.

He found a towel by a sink in the short passageway connected to the office. Daniel checked the bottom drawers of a metal cabinet that almost reached the ceiling, then pushed a chair next to the cabinet, stood on it with great effort and checked the top drawers. Inside one was a rectangular bag containing bandages, dressings, plasters, a packet bearing the words *Sterilising Salts*, vials, sticky tape, scissors and safety pins.

Sometimes when his uncle visited, they would practice dressing imaginary wounds in the living room. Daniel had never thought he'd have to do it for real.

He slid off the chair, slumped to the floor and tore his shirt open. Pressing the towel against his wound, he tore open the packet of sterilising salts with his teeth. He cried out as he spread the salts across the wound, counting his breaths as he tried to take his focus off the pain. He took the towel from his chest, grabbed the largest dressing he could find and pressed it to the wound. He cut some sticky tape and fixed the dressing in place. Rolling a thick bandage around his chest, he fixed it in place with more tape and some safety pins.

Dragging himself back over to the chair, he tried to stand. His vision was blurry with tears as he looked over at the commander's body. What was he going to do? So many questions raced through his mind. He shifted, swivelling the chair round to face the desk. On top of the desk Daniel saw a crumpled poster of a large upside-down triangle; a smaller, black triangle formed the peak of the pyramid at the bottom. Above the shape were the words:

THE ANTI-CONSUL MOVEMENT NEVER SLEEPS. IT WILL FIGHT AGAINST THE CONSUL AND ALL GOVERNMENTS UNTIL THE END OF THE WORLD. WE ALL DESERVE TO BE FREE FROM WANT. FREE FROM COMPUTER CHIPS AND NEVER-ENDING SURVEILLANCE. FREE FROM THOSE WHO OUT OF NOTHING BUT PRIDE AND ARROGANCE CALL THEMSELVES THE RULING CLASS. JOIN US AND YOU

WILL NEVER FEEL SUBJUGATION AGAIN.

Daniel had not heard the word 'subjugation' before. He pressed his hands down on the edge of the desk and stood up. He decided to take the bandages and a coat left on a hook behind the door. Daniel looked at the soldier's body. He felt like he was going to throw up. He turned his head away, terrified of the fact he had just killed someone. *Is this what my uncle felt like when he killed someone in war?*

Daniel put the coat on. It was way too big for him, almost down to his ankles, but it would hide his wound and the flintlock he had recovered from the soldier's body. It felt even heavier this time. He slid the pistol into an inside pocket, buttoned up the coat and pushed open the door to the station.

He looked around, waiting for the door to click shut behind him before shuffling towards the cleaning storeroom. He gripped the coat, checking all of its buttons were done up. He walked over to the door through which the soldiers had taken Ketch and, taking a deep breath, pushed it open. Neither Ketch nor the guards were inside. In the dim light, he could see ageing mops and brushes, and there was a strong smell of chemicals.

Daniel stepped out of the room. Jassk's station buzzed with people returning home, for beyond the glass windows above the platform the light was fading. He decided it was too dangerous to look around the station for clues as to Ketch's whereabouts given the small case of the dead Jasskian captain in the guardroom, so Daniel walked out of the station, thinking that if by some small chance Ketch was still alive and had escaped, he would have returned to the hotel. He recalled the name *Yavos* from the large, tacky sign above its entrance. Retracing his steps was difficult, but not impossible. He also remembered the surveillance cameras in Jassk's transport-pods. Daniel stole a folded rectangular piece of black material from a cloth merchant's stall when he turned to talk to a customer. He found it odd the City Watch had not gone and demanded the merchant produce a permit or forced him to go to Market Dome yet. Reaching a transport-pod platform, Daniel covered his face with the black cloth and took a pod to Market Dome. Removing the cloth, he walked down the main thoroughfare, asking people every so often for directions to the hotel.

After a long while searching, he found himself outside it. No one was in the lobby, so he rang the bell on the reception desk. Taking a seat in a large wicker chair, he thought about what to do next. Looking up at the fan swirling above the lobby, Gressil popped into his mind. Gressil! He was the only one Daniel knew in this city, and the only one to date with a known relationship to the Jasskian Guards. It seemed so simple: he would go to the shop, threaten him and demand he discover Ketch's whereabouts from the City Watch.

Clasping the flintlock underneath the guard's coat,

Daniel tried to stand up, but his body did not obey and he fell forward, knocking his head against the lobby floor.

When he came to, he was lying in a bed, with light streaming in through the cracks in a blind above his head. His chest still felt sore, but less than before, though his head was pounding. He was wearing a dark blue T-shirt, and wondered where his own T-shirt and the rubber belt were. He pulled up the T-shirt to see that the bandages had been changed.

'How are you feeling?' said a voice.

He looked up to see Niya, Ketch's friend from the hotel. 'What did you ...?'

'We, that is, my husband and I, thought it best to sew up that nasty hole in your chest while you were out,' Niya said, 'but before that we restored your broken rib with a repair mecha. It will take a few days to stop hurting while the muscles heal. The stitches will dissolve.'

'Thank you,' Daniel said.

'Oh, don't thank *me*,' the woman said. 'It was my husband Tarnat who saw you keeled over on our floor.'

'I'm sorry about that.'

'Don't worry, we just don't want customers dying in the lobby! Or anyone, for that matter!' Niya winked.

'Well, thank you.' Daniel smiled back. 'Do you have my rubber belt? I was wearing it across my shoulder.'

Niya did not reply.

'How did you get that wound in your chest?' she said. 'You had a guard's coat on when you came back yesterday. And why isn't Ketch with you?'

'I fell on a railing outside,' Daniel lied. 'And I found the coat abandoned in a skip.'

'So your wound had nothing to do with *this*?'

She took out the flintlock, bullet bag, powder flasks and measurer from a drawer in the bedside cabinet and laid them on top. Daniel caught a glimpse of the black rubber belt in the drawer.

'Listen, I'm sorry, I wasn't completely truthful. It's just that if anyone knew why I was really here, I would be in big trouble.'

'You *do* know these things are banned in the city? And a boy like you shouldn't be using one.'

'But that's just it, I haven't used one ... I mean, Ketch gave it to me to use only in self-defence, and it saved my life. Not through shooting it, that is. Anyway, I'm looking for a certain jewel that Ketch believes is in the city. As you probably know, he is wanted for a crime by the City Watch, a ridiculous charge, so we each carry a gun to protect ourselves.'

'So, where is he?'

'He was shot by guards at the railway station. They dragged his body away when they arrested me. I ... I don't even know if he's alive.'

'The consul and his soldiers will pay for that,' she said with fire in her eyes. 'We must find out if Ketch is still alive.'

After a short silence, she continued.

'I took the liberty of putting the soldier's coat you borrowed out with the rubbish. Here, have some food, you must be hungry.'

Niya held out a tray containing some green bread rolls.

'Thank you,' Daniel said, picking one up gingerly.

He bit into it. It tasted sweet, and then a sourness came through while he chewed. Daniel could not identify whether the roll's filling was vegetable or meat and thought it rude and pointless to ask. Besides, he was so hungry unidentified alien food had to do.

As Niya turned to place the tray on the bedside table, the short sleeve of her shirt raised to reveal a tattoo of an upside-down triangle.

'That's the sign of the Anti-Consul Movement. Are you part of that?' Daniel asked.

'Oh *that*. Yes, we are,' she whispered. 'The consul's scum and so are the Council ministers.'

'Forgive me for saying this, but what will the soldiers do if they find out Ketch stayed here?'

'If he is still alive, he won't talk. Ketch is a fighter.'

Daniel got up from the bed.

'Wait, you should rest! Your wound has not yet healed completely!'

'Thank you, and your husband. I promise I'll come back and return the favour one day.'

'You need to rest, Daniel!'

'I can't. I have to find out if Ketch is still alive, and I don't want you risking yourselves. I'm the reason he was shot.'

'You have to rest,' said Niya. 'Tomorrow one of our people will be able to help you.'

'I can't wait until tomorrow!' Daniel said. 'I feel this all happened because of me. I need to know if he's still alive.'

'Our whole family cares about Ketch. If he's alive, we have spies who will be able to find out where he's being held. Leave it to us and rest for now. I'll check on you in the evening,' she smiled, switched off the light and left the room.

In some pain, Daniel got out of bed. He took the rubber belt from the drawer and put it over his head and onto one shoulder. He fastened the flintlock, powder flasks, measurer and bullet bag to his belt. Daniel pulled up the blinds and looked out of the window. There was a fire ladder to the street below within reach from the window. He opened the window and made his way down the ladder to the street.

Chapter 10

FOUND

Daniel was sure he was lost. He had taken a transport-pod to the central market and followed the original trail back towards Gressil's shop, but all of the streets in the market district had melded into one. He looked for where the merchants sold jewels, Rare Street and the big red sign of Gressil's shop, but no luck. He stopped to catch his breath next to some market stalls on which rested cages containing live animals, some of which he had never seen before. His chest felt tight, but wasn't so painful. He thought of Niya and how kind she had been. Maybe one day he could return with a gift from home. He had to find a way to get back first.

Daniel asked directions from a passing trader pushing a cart piled high with hi-tech parts. He was on the wrong side of the central market, apparently. To reach Rare Street, he had to walk back and follow the signs to the Jewel Sector. This news, though disheartening, gave him a focus. If Gressil was there, he may know something about Ketch's arrest.

He headed back through the streets to the Central Station entrance and the main market below. By then, the sun was beginning to dip below the top of the building. Looking up, he saw signs to the consul's palace and the Mountain

Gate, and one for the Jewel Sector. He would have to be quick if he were to catch Gressil before he closed shop.

He began to jog, weaving past people in the city's main square below the Central Station. Reaching a street that ran away from the square, he read the sign: *Mytan Street*. Turning back, he almost ran into a hover-car coming down the street. The driver swerved and just avoided hitting a trader selling pasties from a cart, before speeding on.

Daniel glanced at a clock above a watch shop: ten minutes to six. Panic struck. Had he really been walking around for that long? He started to run, looking down the side streets for the big red sign of Gressil's, becoming more and more frantic when he couldn't find it. He saw another clock; it was now five minutes to six.

'Where is Gressil's?!' Daniel shouted.

'Over there,' replied a woman carrying a baby, and twitched her head to the right.

'Thank you!'

He hurried down the street she had indicated and saw the sign. There was no time to waste, so he decided to go in through the second door to surprise Gressil. Feeling the edge of the heavy metal door, he was able to prise it open with his fingertips. With one hand on his gun, he scaled the dark steps towards the treacherous merchant's office. Sneaking into the display room, which was unoccupied, he heard the sound of voices coming from the back room. On the floor was a smashed glass and a green stain which he assumed was from a whistberry sherb.

Suddenly, it went quiet. Daniel listened carefully, and then with a tremendous bang the door was thrown open against the wall and men armed with spears flooded the room and surrounded him. Daniel froze. A lieutenant of the guard emerged with the same number of pips on his shoulder as the one at the station.

'You are under arrest by orders of the consul. Take him.'

Daniel felt a strong blow to the head, and falling to the floor, everything went black.

'But, Mummy, where is Daniel?'

'I don't know, sweetheart ... We'll find him.'

'I hope he's not hurt. Why hasn't he called?'

'Come on, let's keep looking.'

Daniel woke. He had been dreaming of his mother and sister, hearing their voices. He was blinded by a bright light shining in his eyes. He stroked the back of his head. The soldiers had given him a painful bump. He touched his neck. The chain from his mother was missing! He realised he was lying on the cold, hard stone floor, and with his eyes adjusting to the brightness, he could just make out the bottom of some iron bars in front of him, and a pair of black boots. He heard scribbling, and then it stopped. The light moved up and the boots walked away, clacking harshly on the stone. He heard the jangling of keys and then silence, and darkness returned.

'Nice of you to drop by,' croaked a voice to his right.

'Ketch! Is that you?'

Daniel got up, feeling his way towards the source of the voice until his hands were up against the bars between the two cells.

'Sorry to disappoint you. Still alive and kicking. They patched me up.'

'Why did they fix you? I thought they didn't care.'

'It seems they are going to use me as an example to deter Jassk's good citizens from any foolishness. Put me on trial, that type of thing. Then they'll execute me.'

'How long have you been here?'

'Since the scuffle at the station. How did you escape?'

Daniel paused. He did not want to talk about it.

'Long story,' he said.

'Are you all right?' Ketch asked.

'I'm fine,' Daniel replied. 'Somehow we've got to get out of here.'

'Shh, not so loud. I've been thinking about that. The jailer isn't the conversational type and I haven't yet noticed anything useful near the cells.'

'But there must be something we can use,' Daniel whispered, and walked over to the front of his cell, feeling the lock with his hands. 'Do you have any powder left?'

'Good thinking, but they took everything from me.'

'You have any ideas?'

'Well, I've noticed that the cell doors have a mechanical lock.'

'And the jailer carries the keys,' Daniel added, moving back to rest against the bars between their cells, eager to hear Ketch's plan.

'Exactly. He comes to check on us every 30 minutes. Now, I was banking on grabbing him when he peers through the bars with that infernal torch and relieving him of the said set of keys.'

'But how come you haven't tried that before?'

'The man is obese, so if he was facing me I would not be able to get my arm around him.'

'So what's your plan?'

'You're going to help me get the keys. I think if I grab the jailer during his next check, you could grab the keys from the side of his belt.'

'But how will we get him close enough?'

'I'll call for him when he arrives. With any luck, he'll come near the bars and shine his torch in my cell. When he's past the front of your cell, I will sneak up to reach through the bars and grab hold of his neck. Then you'll grab the keys, and pull his ankles so that he rolls onto the floor. I'll then squeeze his neck until he passes out, and you'll unlock both the doors.'

'What if I can't reach the keys? And do you have enough

strength to make him unconscious? What if he screams out, alerts the other guards?'

'I'm fine. He won't. It'll work.'

'How can you be sure?' Daniel asked.

'It *has* to work,' Ketch replied. 'Now we just wait until the jailer's next rounds.'

Daniel thought the plan seemed a little desperate, but he couldn't think of a better option. If they were going to do this, they would have only one chance.

'Okay, be ready!' Ketch whispered after around 20 minutes had passed and the clomping of boots could be heard.

The light of a torch could be seen high in the far left corner of the dungeon, juddering up and down with each step the jailer made down the steps.

'I know you!'

Daniel jumped as Ketch shouted towards him.

'You're that little wretch who took my gun at the market. Come here! Wait till I get my hands on you!'

The light stopped and then flashed across Daniel's eyes, blinding him for a moment, before resting on Ketch, who was holding the bars between their cells with a look of demented anger on his face. The light, still focused on Ketch, began to move closer.

'Yeah, you! I dare ya, come near the bars. I'll throttle ya!'

'Quiet, you scum! Give up the act, we know you and the

boy are friends,' a voice shouted, heavy with phlegm.

The light moved past the front of Daniel's cell and he could now make out the enormous size of its holder. The jailer stopped in front of Ketch's cell, but the torch was no longer fixed on its occupant.

'Where are you?'

The light moved back and forth across the cell.

'Arghhh!'

Ketch had sprung from below and thrust his arms through the bars, grabbing hold of the jailer's thick forearms and pulling them hard.

'Quick, the keys!' Ketch said.

'I'll get you for this. Guards! Guards!' the jailer yelled.

'Forget the keys. Shut him up!' Ketch said, pulling the jailer's fingers back and causing him to drop the torch.

'Arghh! They are ... trying to escape!' the jailer struggled.

'Wait, I can do this,' Daniel said as he reached for the keys, removing them from a hook on the fat man's belt.

'Shut him up! Now!' cried Ketch.

Daniel threw the keys into his cell and lunged for the torch. It was just beyond his reach.

'Guards! Get here now!'

With the blood pumping through his veins, Daniel lay flat on the stone floor of his cell and stretched with all his might. He rolled his fingers over the torch and picked it up. The jailer struggled, pulling one arm free from Ketch's grasp.

'Help, now!' Ketch said.

'For the love of Melithusa ... guards!' the jailer shouted.

He pulled on the jailer's other arm and then punched him in the mouth with his free hand.

Daniel brought the heavy torch down on the jailer's thick skull with all the force he could muster. The huge man stopped screaming for a moment.

'Hit him again!' Ketch said, and Daniel did as instructed.

The jailer slumped to the floor, out cold.

'Quick, let's go!'

Daniel darted back to get the keys and went to open his cell door, getting the right one on the third try. He unlocked the door to Ketch's cell and they crept up the steps together. At the top, Ketch peered round a door left ajar by their captor and looked down the corridor. The coast was clear, for the moment. The office within had lockers with eye scanners and key-fob locks; the jailer's set of keys included a key-fob.

Daniel checked the clipboard on the desk for clues as to where their personal effects were being held. One entry read "Ketch Raynott-24". He could not see his name, but there were two lockers marked 'Unnamed'.

'Know what we need? Come on, give me a hand,' Ketch said as they dashed back to the dungeon.

Picking up the jailer was impossible, so they had to drag his body across the dungeon floor and up the steps, panting heavily. When they eventually got back to the office, they stood in front of locker 24.

'Quick, open his eye,' Ketch said.

Daniel pressed open the sweaty man's right eyelid as they struggled to keep his unconscious body upright.

'SCANNING ... GRANTED. PRESS KEY ON MAGNETIC CIRCLE.'

Daniel used the fob from the set of keys and the locker door clicked open. Ketch grabbed his belongings and then checked his wrist.

'They haven't reset the code completely, which is what they do to convicted prisoners.'

Daniel looked at the green digits on Ketch's wrist. They read '000000000333'.

'I assume it's so that in the event that I escape, they can track me if I spend altins.'

'Better not spend any then,' Daniel said, checking the *Unnamed* lockers again.

They moved the jailer level with locker 25 and opened his eye again. With a press of the fob the locker clicked open. It was lucky his stuff was in this one. The rubber belt, the gun, shot, powder flasks, measurers were all there. And Daniel's neck chain. He picked them up, fastened the chain around his neck and threw the belt over one shoulder. They loaded and primed their flintlocks as quickly as they could, and then as stealthily as possible sped down the corridor, not wanting to wait until the fat jailer regained consciousness. They passed a courtyard with a fountain. Daniel felt more confident about their escape upon seeing sunlight streaming down onto the water's surface.

'Wait! Someone's coming,' Ketch said as he stretched his head round the next corner. 'One, two, three, four ...' he whispered.

'What are you doing?' Daniel asked.

'Five, six, seven ... Counting steps. I'll—'

CRASH.

In a flash Daniel was round the corner. Ketch feared the worst. To Ketch's surprise, Daniel, torch in hand, was standing over the guard, who was now lying unconscious on the floor.

'Daniel, why didn't you let me handle it?'

'Got the job done, didn't I? Let's go.'

They ran down the corridor, trying not to make a sound, until they reached a set of large wooden doors reinforced by metalwork. There was a smaller door within one of the larger doors. Ketch tried the handle, but it was locked.

'Try the keys,' he suggested.

Daniel fumbled through the keys on the metal ring, trying the largest one first. It fit. As the door opened, bright light blinded him as Ketch walked ahead down the stone steps. After his eyes adjusted, Daniel saw that they were above another square, smaller than the one near the station. He hoped no one had seen them escape. There was no time to waste and the jewel had to be found soon, now that Ketch, a "Public Enemy", was meant to be in a jail cell in the city, and Daniel would be hunted for a series of crimes, one far worse than those Ketch was accused of. He thought about what would happen if his mum knew. There were indeed worse things than spending the night in a cell.

Ketch stopped to catch his breath.

'Okay, so where is the jewel again?' Daniel asked. 'The consul's palace? If it's being stored elsewhere or it has been sold on, it could be anywhere in the city, or even beyond.'

'No, it's here,' Ketch said. 'The consul would not part with such finery. It's likely on display or hidden in a safe place in his private quarters in the palace. I'll show you how to get there.'

Chapter 11

A CLIMB

'Here we are.'

Ketch pointed up at a huge cliff face, on top of which were the pale-yellow stone walls of the palace.

'The only way to get there is up,' he said.

'You've *got* to be joking,' Daniel replied angrily.

'To find the jewel you need to get into the consul's palace. It's guarded at the gates and the walls. The gates are locked to all but those who have appointed business with the palace, and they need a password from the palace to gain entry. The password is changed after each official visit or delivery. You can't distract the soldiers and creep in, as they are allowed to talk to no one; they only open the gates when the correct password is spoken. Patrols check for distractions so that the guards stationed at the gates and the walls never have to move from their posts to investigate. Trust me, this is the only way in.'

'Are you nuts? Better just to kill ourselves now.'

'I'll have to sit this one out I'm afraid,' Ketch said. 'If I'm caught climbing the palace walls I'll be executed for certain. Plus, everyone is after me right now.'

'They are after me as well if you haven't noticed!' Daniel

exclaimed.

'For stealing, you might only get your hand chopped off, as it's your first serious offence. Well, second, after breaking out of jail with me,' Ketch said.

'There must be another way in,' Daniel said.

'Believe me, there isn't. Unless you have a barcode on your arm and are registered for official business that day.'

Daniel thought for a minute.

'Can't you hack and reprogramme your barcode, and then we can pretend to be traders the consul has requested?'

'Still, we don't have the password, and our faces will be one of the most popular things on public monitorvisors around Jassk when they know we have escaped. We don't have much time. I'm sorry to say, but this is it. If you want the jewel it is. Time to make a decision. You might not have another chance to get the parts for the portal generator to get you home.'

Daniel looked up at the cliff face. They couldn't buy climbing equipment, as the purchase would be tracked when Ketch used his barcode. Also, he was afraid of heights, although this seemed like suicide for anyone. Daniel wondered why Ketch, a Delvidran, was going to all this trouble to help him return home yet now was leaving him by himself. *Maybe he is a spy. Maybe they all are spies.* He started to wonder if Ketch was working for the king. *Or was he trying to get his hands on the pieces needed to fix the portal machine to find his wife on Earth?* Daniel began to get paranoid that maybe even Alpona knew more about Ketch's intentions than him. Even if Ketch and the king got to Earth, he thought, they couldn't hope to attack it without guns, ships and planes at least as modern as those of the Americans. They only really had the Radiants. Whatever the truth was, Daniel thought to himself maybe he should keep a close eye on Ketch whenever he could.

However, for the sake of this blasted jewel and his chance of getting home, Daniel knew he had to try. And it was worth it to see his mum and sister again.

Daniel took a deep breath. 'Okay, let's go.'

They walked down one of the side roads to the foot of the cliff.

'It looks like you can get a sure foothold here,' Ketch said. 'It won't be so bad when you've climbed for a while.'

'Easy for you to say!'

'The cliff narrows nearer the top. Use your eyes. Look, then place your feet carefully and pull yourself up with your hands. When you reach the halfway point, you will notice the rock is less jagged.'

'Yes, I see that.'

Peering up, Daniel could make out the vague black figures of birds flying above the ramparts built into the rock.

'The way in is through the latrine sluice in the walls,' Ketch said. 'It's large enough for a man, so you should have no trouble.'

'I don't know what I'm looking for even if I do get in!'

'It's a large cut green jewel, about the size of your fist. Do you know how to get back to the hotel? It's the Yavos, remember?'

'Yes, I do ...'

'I'll wait there for you. Sneak out of the palace any way you can and take a transport-pod to Market Dome. Follow the main thoroughfare north and turn onto Rowkan Street. You'll see it. If you don't make it to the hotel this evening, I'll assume you've been captured and will find out where you're being held. It may take a while for a jailbreak, but I'll do my best.'

'*Your best!?* What if they cut my hand off?'

'Don't worry, they won't do that before you're tried in court, and it'll take a few days at least before they bring you to trial. I'll have you out before then. Good luck. You'll be fine. Just don't look down!'

Daniel wasn't sure about this, but there seemed to be no other option. He put his foot on the rock and started to climb.

The wound from the soldier's spear throbbed so that every movement was like a knife pricking at his chest. There was a slight breeze now and the weight of the gun felt heavier. Taking deep breaths, trying to block out the pain, he knew he could give in to his terror at any moment. A thousand school litter picks would be better than this. All he could do was focus on his breathing and on every move upwards he made. If there was a god, he hoped they would not let him fall.

He paused to rest for a moment, like he had done several times before. Looking up, he knew he was getting closer, as the latrine sluice was gradually getting bigger. He also heard the chilling cawing of what he thought must be crows above him, though he could not see them.

The breeze picked up into sporadic winds strong enough to cause trouble for his ascent, and the climb became slower and more difficult. The dark shapes re-emerged, flying down off the ramparts. He wasn't far from the sluice, maybe a hundred feet or so, when they struck him with a flurry of beaks and talons.

Daniel shouted out, surprised by the attacks. Amidst the disorientating flapping of wings, his hands hurt trying to keep a firmer grip. His feet began to slip. He knew the crows or one more strong gust of wind would be enough to shake him from the cliff and send him falling to certain death.

He desperately tried to find a better foothold, blood dripping from his forehead. He spotted a long horizontal crack in the rock face just above where his feet kept sliding. Hooking one foot and then the other into the crack, with all the strength left in his legs, Daniel straightened himself against the cliff face and pushed his hands up against the rock until they found holds. Then, he lowered one hand, adjusted the rubber belt on his shoulder and took out the pistol that he had tucked into his trouser belt.

A beak snapped at his hand, causing him to yell out in pain. Swinging at the bird with his free hand, Daniel deterred it for a few seconds, just long enough to enable him to balance on the ledge, his legs taking his weight. He cocked the flintlock's hammer back, aimed in the centre of the swirling cloud of birds and fired. The shot clipped the wing of one of his attackers, and unable to maintain flight, the crow plummeted to the ground below. The other crows paid attention, and started frantically flapping their wings to get away, scared by the noise.

Teetering on the ledge, with his feet still taking his weight, Daniel feared he would soon lose his balance and slip. He saw the crows fly up beyond the sluice, cawing as they returned to the ramparts. He tucked the pistol through his belt and breathed in, blood trickling from his hand and forehead. He wiped his brow and carried on with the climb.

He soon made it to the sluice, and pulling himself into the square hole cut into the rock, he collapsed from exhaustion. For a few moments he lay at the edge, feeling the pain beneath his bandage and the murderous winds blowing into the sluice. He looked above him and saw that the gap was lined with stone to reinforce it against the rock. It must have been the main sewage exit before it was replaced with a new system. *Ketch was right, there must be a way in through here.* With a struggle, Daniel got back on his feet, and stepping across the channel once used for the overflow, followed a walkway into the darkness beyond. Stumbling around in the dark, he continued on the walkway farther into the bowels of the rock. He was thankful that the passage did not stink of ages-old waste from the palace as he had imagined.

It was not long before he could see a small shaft of light coming from the ceiling of the sewers. Moving closer, Daniel could see a metal ladder and he climbed up into the palace. Bringing his eyes up over the level of the floor, he checked to see if anyone was in the room. It was deserted. He climbed into what looked like a workroom for those who had worked on the sewer. There were plastic overalls hanging from a rack on one wall, with a row of heavy-duty boots below them. An assortment of mechanical contraptions, presumably used to clean or unclog the sewers, lay strewn over the table and shelves.

He picked up a knife from the desk and inched open the door. Beyond was a spiral stone staircase that led up to a hallway from where he could hear what he thought were metal clanging noises, then someone swearing. Moving carefully so as not to attract any attention, he neared a large set of swing doors in the right-hand wall. Pressing himself against the wall next to the doorframe, curiosity got the better of him, and he pushed the door ajar and peered in. Inside were several large windowless kitchens, one after another through more swing doors. At the end of the first, pacing between huge pans from which bubbled clouds of steam stood a platoon of chefs. Above the clamour of the kitchens, Daniel heard one chef mention to another that some guards were investigating a loud crack heard beneath the palace walls. Another voice said a piece of wall had broken off and the place was falling apart.

He decided to creep past, and holding his breath, he tiptoed across the doorway when the cooks were scurrying between pots. No one saw him. Daniel made his way to the door at the end of the hall. Trying it as quietly as he could, he found it opened out into another corridor with a number of doors on each side, and a spiral staircase to his right. Assuming these to be the living quarters of the palace staff, he took the stairs to where he hoped the consul lived. No sooner had he put one foot on the steps than he heard laughter and voices. Someone was coming down the staircase.

Panicking, he hid in a small gap behind the last few steps.

'If those fools have any more wine, they're going to burst!'

'If they have any more food, they're going to burst!'

The owners of the two voices reached the bottom of the staircase. Daniel could see four shiny black shoes. A bell rang several times from the kitchens. One pair of shoes stopped and the other moved away, before returning after a few seconds.

'Take this to the top table. Let's see if they do, ha-ha!'

The pair of shoes nearest to Daniel turned and climbed the staircase, and when the other pair had turned and marched into the kitchens, he got up from his hiding place and crept up the staircase. He took the knife from his belt and held it in front of him. Each step felt like an eternity. He was sure someone would come down, and then he would be discovered and thrown back in jail, or worse.

After a few more steps, the sound of footsteps returned and sent a chill down his spine. He stopped for a second, overcome with panic. The footsteps were getting louder, and were coming from below him! With no choice but to run up the rest of the steps, Daniel prayed that he would make it to the top without being trapped.

He was met with a new hall and new hope. He had made it! With his heart pounding like a drum, he looked round for a hiding place. Suits of armour, fixed upright, each grasping a spear in their mailed right fist, lined both sides of the hall, with a huge window behind the left row. There was nowhere to hide. Panicking, Daniel darted behind the closest suit of armour. Farther down the hall, someone walked to the top of the staircase carrying a tray on which sat the carcass of an animal Daniel could not identify. Suddenly, the tray fell, clanging on the stone floor.

'Get out of the way, will you?' a voice shouted angrily.

Peering over the suit of armour's shoulder, Daniel could see the person coming up the stairs.

'I didn't see you!' another voice said.

'You should have heard me, you idiot! Help me pick these up. Take this in, I'll take that, and we'll say no more about it.'

The waiter turned back with a huge tray of potatoes and walked out of the hall. The sound of footsteps on the stone staircase was growing fainter. Over the suit of armour's other shoulder, Daniel examined the exits at the far end of the hall. Assuming the consul's private quarters were somewhere above the dining hall – and that was rather an assumption, as they could be anywhere – he looked for a staircase. Aside from the opening, there was a shiny black door. He crept out from behind the armour, dashed over and tried the handle. It opened, and led to a small room with a lift.

Moving closer, to Daniel's surprise a mechanical arm jolted out from one of the panels in the ceiling and pushed what looked like a scanner towards his eye.

'PLEASE PLACE YOUR EYE OVER THE SCANPOINT.'

The electronic voice disturbed him. His eye was not accepted, and since there were only buttons for levels below this floor he did not believe this was the way to the consul's apartments.

As he took a step back, the mechanical arm retracted and shot up into the ceiling. He pushed the black door ajar to check if anyone was around and slipped through the opening and hid. A girl with red hair and dark skin wearing formal clothes was running down the hall towards another black door. As she opened it, Daniel checked no one else was coming, drew the knife from his belt and sneaked through the door.

Ahead of him was another lift with a scanner in front of the girl's eyes. The lift shaft continued above this level. He heard the same instruction from the electronic voice, the girl placed her eye over the scanner and the doors opened. In a flash, Daniel grabbed her and jumped through the doors, placing one hand over her mouth.

'Close the doors!' he instructed.

At that moment, an older woman entered the room, dressed in clothes resembling those of a lady-in-waiting from Daniel's history books. Seeing the struggle, she dashed towards them.

'Now!' Daniel shouted, prodding the knife against the girl's throat.

Terrified, the girl pressed a button.

'RETINAL VERIFICATION ACCEPTED.'

The doors closed.

'To the consul's quarters,' Daniel said. 'If you try to trick me, I'll put this knife through your neck.'

The girl pushed another button and the lift began to climb.

'If you scream, I'll do the same. If you answer my

questions, I'll let you go. You understand?'

The girl nodded, tears trickling down her face. Daniel took his hand from her mouth and the knife away from her neck. The girl pushed herself as far away from him as the space in the lift allowed.

'The jewel. Great green thing about the size of my fist,' Daniel said. 'You have to show me where it's kept.'

'I don't have to do anything you say!' the girl shouted, sniffling. 'I recognise you; you're the boy from the prison break. Your face is on all of the monitorvisors in Jassk.'

'If you want to keep breathing, then show me where the jewel is.'

'Who says I know where it is?'

'*I* think you know. You're too young to be a serving girl and those are some pretty fancy clothes.'

'How do you expect to get out after I show you the jewel? The palace has guards on every level,' the girl said.

The lift stopped and the doors clicked open to reveal an ornate hall. Daniel pushed the girl forwards.

'Show me where it is,' he demanded.

With the knife held in front of him, he followed her through more decorated hallways with more suits of armour until they reached a tall, dark wooden door.

A scanner like the one for the lift was built into the wall. The girl stretched on her tiptoes and placed her eye over the mechanism. No comment came from the machine, but he heard a click. He pushed the girl through the door and followed.

'There! Satisfied?'

With fresh tears filling her eyes, she pointed towards a display case in the centre of a square room lined with pictures and chairs. Through the glass Daniel could see the jewel. Green and shimmering with light from above it, it was cut in the shape of a pear, and was indeed as big as his fist.

'Come on,' he said, prodding the girl forwards to the display, knife ready. 'Do not move.'

He picked up a chair from the side of the room and with great strain sent one of its legs crashing through the glass. The girl screamed. An alarm began to sound as he snatched the jewel. Finding it too big to fit in his pockets, he dashed for the door with it in his palm. The entrance had locked behind them. Amidst the intermittent wails of the alarm, he heard the "ding" sound of the lift arriving, then loud thumping on the locked door that sent him reeling back around the room. In the opposite corner was another door with another scanner.

'Open this door or I will kill you before they reach us!'

'No! I would rather die!'

Frustrated, Daniel ran back and grabbed her. With the girl beginning to sob, he pressed her face towards the scanner on the wall. The door clicked open. Releasing the girl, he escaped just as the guards and lady-in-waiting burst into the room. They were led by a bald man, his shirt bearing the insignia of the consul.

Daniel ran down the stone corridor as fast as his tired legs would carry him. Behind him, Daniel noticed the girl followed him, and was now struggling to lift a spear that made up one of the corridor's many displays with suits of armour. The door at the end led to a dark metal walkway. Lights came on above him as he ran towards it.

Beyond, below an enormous metal dome, was a small black airplane with a ladder leading up to the cockpit. Daniel rushed over, climbed the ladder and inspected the controls. There were so many buttons and indicators.

Suddenly, he felt a sharp pain in his shoulder. Clutching the wound, he turned around. The girl was at the top of the ladder, pointing a bloodied spear straight at him, her eyes gleaming with fury and tears. He moved to push the ladder from under her, but she leapt into the cockpit. Hearing boots clapping on the metal floor of the gangway in the other room, Daniel began to press buttons and flip switches in the desperate hope of starting the plane's engine.

'You'll pay for this,' the girl said, standing on the co-pilot's seat, pointing the spear down at his back, 'for threatening me and stealing that jewel. It's my mother's.'

'I'm sorry,' Daniel said, groaning from the pain in his shoulder, 'but I have to take it to get home.'

The girl lunged at him with the spear, but Daniel dodged

it just in time and the spearpoint found the plane's dashboard, sending sparks flying.

The guards entered and ran towards the ladder. Avoiding the dashboard's crackling electricity, Daniel flipped another random switch and the whole room began to shake. Then the dome above broke apart, opening outwards like petals on a large black flower. Altinor's sun became a bright wall of light that hit the inside of the dome, bouncing off the plane's smooth surface.

With the ladder now knocked to the floor, the more ambitious of the guards leapt onto the nose and wings of the plane as the engines began to fire. Batting off hits to the head from the girl while trapped in the cockpit, Daniel pulled the spear out of the dashboard, pushed down on the control stick and prayed the plane could still fly. The flames shot from the engines towards the floor of the hangar, forcing the guards and their leader to step back. The aircraft rose slowly like a helicopter, and one plane-scaling guard flew off its nose with a loud cry.

Their leader, furious, ordered them to stop, and shouted something to the guards that Daniel could not hear through the bulletproof glass. They rushed over to some controls on the hangar wall and left the bald figure staring at Daniel while fire sparks rained down from the engines. Peering up, the gash in his shoulder throbbing, Daniel saw the dome begin to close again. The plane, however, cleared it, and with a flick of the wrist, he turned the engines to face behind the plane, propelling it forwards. In a flash they were above Jassk's domes and towers, shooting over the streets and city walls until all Daniel could see below was a sea of pale green scrubland. The aircraft shuddered violently, its control stick fighting Daniel the whole time. He was using all of his strength to hold it level, to keep the machine flying. A flash of what looked like lightning crackled across the glass of the cockpit, and the plane dipped suddenly. Daniel's stomach felt like it was being pushed up into his chest. Out of control, the aircraft hurtled like a meteor towards the ground below. In sheer terror, and trying desperately to pull the plane up, with the girl screaming at him and trying to clamber into the front seat, Daniel held on. It was too late. Before he closed his eyes, *before impact*, his sight was flooded by yellow.

Chapter 12

A FALL

Daniel walked up the hill behind the town. Stopping at the top of the road, he looked at the town of Maxwelltown on the opposite riverbank. He entered a large graveyard and passed gravestones and statues. When he reached a certain line of gravestones, he began checking the names. He was curious as to why he had come here, but he felt something leading him to a certain grave.

He stopped. The dark-grey stone in front of him bore the name JOHN SAMUEL MEARNS. There were no dates.

'This is the grave of your great-grandfather,' a voice said. 'A good view for him from here, don't you think?'

Daniel turned around, but no one was there. He looked at the stone for some time, then across the town and the river. He smiled.

'He was a farmer, like your grandfather.'

'Who are you? Are you a farmer too?' Daniel asked the wind, wondering if he was going mad.

'I knew what I wanted to do,' the voice said.

Though the words were vague, they made Daniel happy. He looked at the gravestone again. The sun was shining and despite where he was, everything seemed good.

He looked to the right and saw that the next gravestone read: DANIEL ROBERT MEARNS. BORN 3RD NOVEMBER 1997. DIED 6TH FEBRUARY ... His *own* grave! Daniel didn't want to see any more, but somehow he couldn't bring himself to look away. He was confused there was no year etched into the stone to mark his death ...

With a jolt, Daniel opened his eyes. At first everything seemed blurry, and all he could see was a brown darkness. Trying to move, his legs felt weak and his arms heavy as weights. He touched his forehead and felt something wet and warm. He was bleeding. Daniel wondered if he would now fear the 6th of February each year.

He looked behind him to see a flame of red hair attacking the brown darkness with her feet.

'Wake up!' she shouted.

His shoulder still ached from where she had stabbed him with the spear. He gulped in the stuffy air of the cockpit. The rubber belt was still over his shoulder, but the jewel that he had placed in the footwell had gone.

'Come on, wake up! The plane could explode at any minute!' she screamed.

His eyes darting around, Daniel saw a crack above him through which he could see a tiny speck of light. He began kicking at it with both feet, and soon shafts of light and sand streamed into the cockpit, until eventually the cockpit top flew open. The girl climbed onto what was left of the plane's right wing. Daniel saw that she was carrying a small canvas backpack over her right shoulder.

'Hey! Give me the jewel back!' he said.

'It was my mother's! You stole it!'

Daniel slid gingerly down the side of the shortened wing and into the sand dune below. The girl's right leg sank into the deep sand and she fell, but soon got back up.

'Where'd you get that backpack, anyway?' Daniel shouted.

'The plane, you idiot, the one you crashed. Oh no! This is past the Beam Wall!'

'I'm no idiot! And what's the Beam Wall?' Daniel asked, falling over in the shifting sand.

At that moment the plane exploded, the force blowing him forwards onto the dune. He looked back, past the wreckage that was now on fire, and answered his own question. A few hundred feet or so behind the plane's blazing carcass was an immense beam of blue light stretching horizontally as far as the eye could see. It looked at least four hundred feet high, and there were no breaks in the beam as far as the horizon in both directions.

'My god ... Wait just a minute! I need to ask you something!'

The girl stopped. Daniel saw that she had blood and tears on her cheek as she looked over at the great wall of light. He felt the knife from the palace still tucked into his belt.

'Go away! I'll never get back now ... not unless they find me,' she said.

Daniel scrambled up the next dune, after the girl. Through her tears she shot him an angry look and began to run down the other side. In pursuit, he leapt towards her, trying to get hold of the backpack.

'No! It's all your fault!' she cried.

They flopped about like fish in the sand, pulling on opposite straps of the bag until Daniel eventually wrestled it from her.

'Take it!' she shouted, lying down on the sand. 'It's no use to me now anyway. Don't think my father won't be looking for me, though. And when he finds you ...'

'Who is your father?'

'The consul.'

'I *knew* you weren't a servant's daughter. Listen ...' He crouched down next to her. 'I'm sorry you got roped into this, but I need your mum's jewel to get home.'

Daniel rolled up his sleeve and showed her his arm. The girl got back on her feet.

'You don't have a barcode ... same as me. Are you one of the Chosen?'

Daniel stood up.

'*Chosen*? I promise you, I am not from here. I am from Earth!'

The girl did not look convinced.

163

'You probably just got it removed. Part of the Anti-Consul Movement or something.'

'I came to this world by mistake. It sounds crazy, but I can't get back to my own world unless I collect these pieces for a machine that can open the door home.'

The sun was blazing down on their heads as they stood in silence for a moment.

'What's your name?' he asked.

'Kala. Not that it would help you at all to know.'

'Pleased to meet you, Kala. I'm Daniel. I'll help you get back to your father, but first we have to find a way through that wall. Can you tell me what you know about it?'

'Why should I trust you?'

Daniel looked at the desert stretching immeasurably before them.

'What choice do you have?'

'The Beam Wall was made by the Jasskians to keep desert raiders out of the Jassk's supporting farmlands,' Kala explained. 'It stretches for hundreds of miles, from the Yimel Mountains in the north to the Sea of Melithusa in the south.'

'Are there any gates in the beam, or is it continuous?'

'Unfortunately, there aren't any gates. In Jassk many say that beyond the Wall is nothing but thieves and desert. I know better, though. I have heard that another sea, the Oargrind, lies to the east.'

'How can you know if you've never been?'

164

'I've read about it in books.'

'Well, books aren't always right,' Daniel said. 'We can't go back, so we should head somewhere with water, food and shade. Or just water would be a good start.'

'There is no *we*. I don't want to go with you. You got me into this mess!'

She began to walk off, onto the next dune.

'You don't know where you're going!' Daniel shouted, staying put.

When she did not reply, he looked once more at the jewel shimmering in the midday sun, returned it to the backpack and began to follow her.

'Why don't you slow down for once?' he shouted, slipping in the deep sand a few feet behind Kala.

He looked up at the dunes ahead of him; they seemed to go on forever. The sand on the horizon glistened below disorientating waves of heat.

'Do you see anything?'

Kala stopped.

'No!' she shouted back. 'Only sand.'

Daniel ran up to the top of the dune where she was standing.

'How do you even know the sea is this way?'

'I don't,' she admitted, 'but judging where the sun is, I'm pretty sure we're going in the right direction. The coast must be farther away than I imagined.'

'Well, I don't want your daddy blaming me if you burn before we get there.'

He took the knife from his belt.

'Oh, I know he already does,' Kala said.

With some difficulty, Daniel cut some pieces of fabric from his trousers to make them into shorts and gave one of the ripped pieces to Kala.

'You can wrap it around your head as a bandana.'

'A bandana?'

'You know, like *this*.'

Daniel placed the other piece on his head and tied it at the back. Kala laughed.

'You look *very* good,' she said sarcastically.

She placed her own piece over her head and folded it into a headscarf.

'I heard another part of the portal machine was being carried by someone travelling to a port beyond this Beam Wall,' Daniel said. 'Maybe I'll find some clues if we get through the desert.'

'Look over there!' Kala said, pointing at two or three black specks in the distance. 'Aren't those trees? Maybe there's some water there.'

Daniel climbed to the top of the sand dune and squinted in the bright sunlight.

'I think they are. Well done! Race you there!' he joked.

He hurried down the dune towards the black specks, but

not before checking he still had his gun and the knife from the palace. He could see that Kala was putting some distance between them, and that suited him fine. That way she would not try to get the jewel back and he would not have to take it from her again.

They were soon near the palm trees. Praying out loud that there would be water, Daniel quickened his pace in anticipation. A dry wind blew across the dunes, providing dust and no respite from the heat.

He let Kala stay a good few feet ahead of him. He stumbled across the sand, his makeshift bandana drenched with sweat. Kala, now at the rocky outcrop, cried out something, removed her bandana and dashed out of sight. Reasoning this could only mean there was water, Daniel plodded after her through the deep sand as fast as his tired legs could carry him.

When he reached the outcrop, he heard a different cry. Above them, squawking in the trees, were two great black vultures with ugly bald pink necks. They made strange whispering buzzing sounds, and then, spreading their wings, swooped down on Kala, who was drinking from a shallow pool. Not wanting to wait for them to peck and claw at her while he loaded the flintlock, Daniel leapt and grabbed one of the large birds. Startled, the vulture wriggled free and turned on him, lunging at his face with its long neck. It pecked his bandana loose and it swirled in the wind onto the ground.

Daniel looked over to see Kala kicking at the other vulture. Swinging his fists, he rolled onto the rocky outcrop, dodging the creature. It hissed and lunged again, but Daniel's foot connected with the bird's head just in time. Dazed, the vulture stumbled back for a moment before launching itself again at its prey. Daniel moved quickly to the side and took out his flintlock. The vulture flew past him to the edge of the pool, and as it turned to face him, Daniel dashed forward and clubbed it in the head with the butt of the flintlock. It fell into the water, stunned, while Daniel ran to get the other bird away from Kala. Pistol-whipping the attacker, he managed to get the creature to stop.

With a cut on her forehead and very angry, Kala got up and ran towards the bird, kicking at it. It flew back up into one of the trees. Meanwhile, the other bird was back on its feet and scratching its talons on the rock, hungry for a kill.

Daniel dodged its attack and clubbed it again with the butt of the flintlock, this time hard on its neck. It crumpled and fell to ground with a mournful cry, motionless.

'I think you've killed it,' Kala said.

'Why are these birds attacking us anyway? I thought vultures were scavengers!'

'Vultures? Is that what they're called? Maybe they're desperate. Don't suppose there's much to eat around here.'

Kala went back to the pool to drink. She washed off the dirt and cleaned the small cuts on her face and arms. Daniel stared for a long time at the huge bird below him.

'How come you don't have a barcode?' Daniel shouted, and indicated to his arm.

Kala looked up.

'I told you, remember? I am the daughter of the consul. We are what people call the ruling class. Neither my father nor any of his family has one. We always had servants to organise everything for us. It's the same for all the other leaders on Altinor.'

'Keep an eye on the other bird while I have a drink,' Daniel said.

Kala turned and peered up at the vulture in the tree. It squawked and flew from the branches to the dead vulture, and began to feed on its fallen counterpart.

'Ugh,' Kala said in disgust. 'They must *really* be hungry.'

Daniel lay flat on the ground with his head above the pool and gulped down water. It wasn't that cool, but tasted ever so sweet after their long journey through the desert. He turned and saw the vulture tearing bits of flesh and feather from the other.

'That *is* disgusting,' he said.

It was several minutes before either of them spoke again.

'We can't stay here forever, we have to get to this port, wherever it is,' Daniel said.

'Obviously,' Kala said, rolling her eyes. 'But how are we going to cross the rest of the desert without water?'

They looked to the horizon and saw nothing in any direction but peaks and troughs of the golden, murderous sand. Daniel took the powder flask Ketch had given him and emptied its contents onto the rock that ringed the pool.

'What are you doing?' Kala asked. 'What if we come across more wild animals or savages? How shall we protect ourselves?'

'Some people call anyone who is not like them savages. Besides, we don't have a choice,' he explained, filling the flask with water. 'If we don't take water, we won't live long enough to come across any of those things.'

He replaced the stop on the powder holder, picked up the bandana and folded it once more on his head. Kala rearranged hers so that her hair trickled out of the top.

'If the sun sets in the same direction here as it does on Earth, then I reckon the sea is *that* way.'

He pointed past the palm trees.

'Except it doesn't. If you *were* from Altinor you would have said *that* way,' Kala said, pointing far to the left of the trees. 'Unless you are trying to trick me.'

'You're just like my sister, always thinking I'm trying to fool you.'

'The sun sets in the north. It must be a few hours past midday now, so it's beginning to dip, but towards the mountains beyond the desert, over *there.*'

She pointed towards blue peaks, hazy in the distance.

'So,' Kala continued, 'with the midday sun we've not been going east exactly. That's why now I can see we have to go *this* way.'

'Okay, you're the boss, so long as this is the right direction. I don't want to end up heading back towards the Beam Wall or whatever it is called because you think your daddy will find us more easily.'

'I just showed you the way, didn't I? Do you want to get back to your so-called home or not? I'm the boss, so *you* go first,' Kala said, her eyes flashing with anger.

Chapter 13

FORJAN

The sun had almost completely dipped below the horizon. They had stopped every hour to share the last of the water in Daniel's powder flask, having three drips each per stop, although this discipline felt like it was giving them a false sense of security rather than being of any genuine use.

'Kala, can you see that?'

'See what?'

'Over there.' Daniel pointed to his right. 'Isn't that a house?'

A few paces behind him, Kala stopped.

'Yes, I think it is. We're saved!'

'I hope so.'

He felt groggy from dehydration.

'It can't be more than two miles away. Hard to say exactly, as it seems to blend in with the colour of the sand. Come on!' she said, striding past him.

He dragged his feet out of the deep sand and began to walk as fast as his tired legs would allow. In this wretched desert, this was little more than the pace of a tortoise.

Daniel jolted, hearing a loud noise like the crack of thunder. But there were no clouds in the dusky sky, pink and orange with the setting sun.

Kala stopped and turned round.

'What was that?' Daniel shouted.

'I ... don't know. Let's keep going.'

Daniel checked the backpack's straps were still secure and threw it back over his shoulder. The jewel seemed heavier than before. With one eye on the sky, they continued.

It felt like hours before they reached their destination. The dunes had turned to hard ground cracked with dryness, and dusk had rapidly turned to darkness. Daniel was worried they wouldn't be able to find the building in the gloom of night, but there it was, only feet ahead. A light shone above the ground, suggesting the building might be inhabited. But the light they had used to guide them after dusk was fixed to the roof of the building. There were no lights on inside.

'Look, a water pump!' Kala said excitedly.

She ran along the right side of the house, and with what strength he had left Daniel followed her. He gripped his pistol tightly in case of an ambush in the darkness. Kala moved the pump handle up and down and gulped the water that gushed out.

'My turn,' Daniel said.

He moved the handle and drank as much water as he could. It felt cool on his tongue, and came as a huge relief to his tired body. He splashed some on his face, gasping. When he stopped, he filled his powder flask and then looked up into the gloom. The buildings he could make out were built from a light-coloured stone and stretched along either side of a dusty central thoroughfare. About three hundred feet farther down the track was another light above a building.

'Come on, let's see if anyone's around,' he said.

'They could be pirates or thieves for all you know.'

'You've been reading too many books. This is probably just a quiet town.'

'Too quiet.'

They walked down the track towards the light. *Like moths to a flame*, Daniel thought. He was slightly ahead of Kala, and stopped under the second light.

'Look,' he said, pointing.

He saw Kala's cheeks flush as she saw what lay ahead. They were standing at the top of a cliff, above a myriad of lights coming from the large town in a cove below. The sea, black and immense, loomed beyond. Steep steps cut into the sandy rock led down.

'It's ... beautiful!' Kala said.

'This might be the port Ketch mentioned.'

'I think this is Forjan. I was given a book about it, though I never thought I'd see it with my own eyes.'

'Well, we'll soon find out. I'll ask someone when we get there.'

'Be careful! If they hear I am from beyond the Beam Wall, they may not give us the warmest reception.'

'It'll be fine. Maybe they'll call you a savage, but that's as much as we'll allow.' Daniel smirked.

Kala narrowed her eyes.

'Just don't say you're the consul's daughter,' he added.

'Yeah, someone *else* might think to kidnap me,' Kala grumbled.

'For the last time, I didn't kidnap you! You chased me into the plane with a spear, remember?'

They walked down the long, winding steps to the town, slipping on occasion as the old stone crumbled beneath their feet. Daniel could hear music, faint at first but becoming louder the closer they got.

When they reached the bottom of the steps, they were exhausted. With Daniel still keeping some distance between them, they passed a number of weathered stone buildings and people with equally weathered faces, but jovial.

'Hey there, what are you kids up to?' an old woman asked as she passed by, her smile proudly displaying her remaining three teeth.

Daniel and Kala looked at each other.

'Come on,' Daniel said.

The music now seemed to be pouring out of every building, creating an atmosphere of celebration. They didn't have to go far before the street split into two, each new street running down one side of an immense stone building with columns holding up an elaborate lintel with carvings of

175

various fishing and trading scenes. Its large doors were closed. And no guards. To one side of the building loomed an enormous communications tower and on it dish antennas of various shapes and sizes. Tusks from what he thought could only be some indescribably large walrus were set into the stone on each side of the steps leading up to the building's entrance.

An icy wind picked up. It whistled through the square like a banshee's wail of warning. He and Kala shivered. Across the street to the left of the central structure a number of people were going in and out of a brightly lit wooden building. It seemed strangely out of place amongst the stone buildings surrounding it. A battered great wooden sign hung from a metal pole sticking out of the building's entrance. It read "The Seaspray Inn" in white letters, and creaked back and forth with the wind. Daniel entered; Kala followed, with an angry look on her face.

The interior was filled with people and the constant hum of talking and laughing. Some bad singing could also be heard, drowned out by stories being told by broad-shouldered, red-faced types to groups of smaller, less sunburnt individuals. Everyone grasped great tankards in their hands so tightly it looked as if they would have to be surgically removed. Everyone had currency storers on their wrists.

Daniel and Kala slowly made their way through the

huddled groups to the bar. Luckily their presence did not seem to register with the sottish clientele. Raising his arm to catch the enormous moustachioed barman's attention, Daniel remembered this was his first time in a pub. He had heard stories from Uncle James that they were one of Britain's greatest institutions, but this one was nothing special.

The dark-haired barman flashed him an angry glance and served the others standing at the bar. Daniel kept his hand raised and looked up at the wall behind the bar, where the great jaws of an unidentifiable creature hung, as long as a double-decker bus. There was also an assortment of enormous stuffed fish and skeletons of sea creatures mounted on every spare inch of wall.

'No kids allowed in here!' the barman bellowed.

Daniel turned to see his huge whiskers leaning across the bar.

'We don't want to drink!' Kala shouted over the throng. 'We just want some water and maybe some food. We crossed the desert and are very tired.'

The barman's face twitched; a nervous tick, perhaps. He looked at them long and hard.

'You crossed the Cadaveri Desert? I don't believe you.'

'Look at our clothes and burnt skin,' Kala said.

Some of the characters propped against the bar stopped talking. Their eyes, most of them glassy from Altinor's alcohol, were now fixed on Kala and Daniel.

'I don't believe you, and I don't want the blood on your faces and clothing defiling my inn. Now get out!' the barman shouted.

Kala looked around.

'Like it doesn't look defiled already,' she said sarcastically to Daniel. 'I have an idea. Collapse,' she whispered.

'What?' Daniel said. '*You* collapse.'

'Come on, you're not as important here.'

'Not as important? What are you talking about?'

'Just do it. You want some food, don't you?'

'Didn't they teach you any manners at the palace?'

He acted a drop to the floor, his body crumpling like he had been knocked down by some meathead from school. The barman looked over the bar. Kala was screaming and crying. A few others nearby looked vaguely concerned and some drinks were put down. With a sigh the barman flipped a wooden barrier up and pushed past the drinkers to inspect the scene.

'Sir, please help him!' Kala shouted.

'Korel!' the barman shouted. 'Come here and take this away!'

He lifted Daniel like he was a toothpick and placed his motionless body against the bar.

'Okay, Jhor, keep your hair on. What's all this then?' a well built blonde woman shouted, wearing an apron over her clothes.

Carrying a tray of empty tankards, she bumped her way through the masses from the back of the bar. She was larger than the barman and looked many years younger. She put the tray down, crouched next to Daniel and placed two fingers on his neck.

'Well, he's not dead. We'll sort him out. And what's all *this*?' she said, touching the pistol on Daniel's belt. 'I'll give him some water, tend to his cuts and let him rest.'

'Miss, please,' Kala said, 'he's my friend, I want to stay with him.'

Korel, also picking up Daniel like he was a toothpick, looked down at Kala, her face and clothes caked in dirt. She smiled.

'Looks like you have a few cuts too. All right, come on then. Mind the bar a moment, Jhor.'

Jhor grumbled as Korel, with Daniel over one shoulder and his backpack on her other, led Kala past the revellers, through a swing door at the back of the bar and into a small room with two beds. She laid Daniel on one while Kala sat on the other, slid the backpack off her shoulder and placed it against the side table, then removed the rubber belt, flintlock, flasks and pouches and placed them all on the side table. She checked Daniel's pulse again.

'He'll come to when he's ready,' she said. 'Back in a minute.'

When Korel had left, Daniel opened his eyes.

'Being unconscious is harder than it looks,' he said.

'I wish you really *were* sometimes,' Kala said. 'Shh! She's coming back.'

'Oh, who cares?' Daniel said, staying upright on the bed.

Korel pushed the door open.

'Oh, you woke up! My name is Korel, co-owner of this inn. We moved you here when you passed out at the bar. And those cuts need treating.'

'I'm Daniel. Thank you for all you've done.'

'Well, we can't have people dying in the inn. Bad for business.' She grinned.

She had a large jug of water and some tankards in one hand and some fresh clothing and towels in the other. She set the tankards on a table and laid two sets of clothes and towels on the end of the bed Kala was sitting on. She took a towel, dipped the end of it in some water from the jug and cleaned their wounds. She then set the water jug on the table next to the tankards.

Inspecting Daniel's forehead and Kala's cheek, Korel applied some salve. Daniel showed her the gash in his chest; she redressed it and then wrapped a bandage around his upper body, fixing it in place with safety pins.

'You're a lucky boy, that's quite a deep wound. Whoever stitched it up did a pretty good job, though. The salve will sting, but it helps, I promise. A few days and you will heal fine, and the bruises on your legs will soon fade. The cuts on your faces aren't deep, but they bled a bit. Have a drink of water, wash yourselves, then try those on,' she said, pointing at the pile of clothes. 'They belong to my younger brother and sister and so may not fit perfectly, but that's all we have. I'll bring you some food when I have a moment.'

'We can't thank you enough,' Kala said, taking the jug and a tankard, pouring herself a drink and gulping it down.

Korel winked. 'Be back in a while.'

Daniel stood and pulled up the legs of his trousers. The salve on his chest did sting, but movement was now less painful. His legs had several bruises, most of them yellow in colour. He picked up the rubber belt from the bedside table and placed it over one shoulder and under the other arm. He then checked the backpack. The jewel was still there. He took the jug of water from the table and poured himself a tankard. He drank and drank and refilled and drank some more until he had quenched his thirst.

They washed their faces and limbs with the remaining water and turned away from each other to change. The shirt, trousers and belt were a little on the large side for Daniel, and he put on his shoes that were still filled with grains of sand. He picked up the flintlock, powder flasks and pouches from the side table and fixed them to his belt.

'So, aren't you going to thank me?' Kala said, tightening the belt that held up her new trousers. The clothes made her look more like a regular girl.

'Thank you? For what?'

'*Only* for getting us water, fresh clothes and a place to rest.'

'Yeah, well, *you* didn't have to play dead.'

'It was a team effort.'

'Anyway, I'm tired. I'm going to try to get some sleep.'

'You *do* know my father will be looking for me. He might already have ordered the Beam Wall to be turned off to let him pass to search for me. He and his bodyguards will be on horseback. They could be near the town by now.'

'I'm sure your daddy and his soldiers won't get here until tomorrow at the earliest,' Daniel said, lying back on the bed.

'How do you know?'

'Isn't there anyone other than your dad you know? Other than your palace staff, of course,' Daniel said in a cruel tone.

Kala looked at him for a while. Her eyes were becoming glassy.

'As a matter of fact, *yes*. My aunt and uncle. My father and I visit them in Ao Sirt a couple of times a year.'

'There you go, jabbering on about your dad again. I'm going to sleep,' he said, turning away from her. He wondered if she was going to cry.

'Well, at least my dad cares about me. I know he'll find me as soon as he can. Where's *your* dad, mmm? Doesn't seem like he's in a hurry to find you.'

'Shut up. SHUT. UP.' Daniel could feel the rage building

up inside of him.

'You can't sleep yet,' Kala said, defiant. 'Korel said she would bring us food.'

'I'm sure I'll wake up when she does. Now give me some peace, you spoiled brat.'

Daniel stirred to the sound of the door creaking.

'I hope the clothes fit okay,' Korel said. 'Where's your friend?'

Korel was carrying a tray of sandwiches with indiscriminate vegetable fillings. Daniel didn't really care what they had in them, they looked good. He smiled at her and looked over at the other bed.

'I don't know.'

'Well, she can't have gone far. Probably in the inn somewhere.'

Daniel felt a breeze coming through the open window next to the bed. The backpack with the jewel inside had gone. He stood up.

'I think she's gone!' he said.

'Without even saying goodbye?' Korel said. 'Are you really friends?'

'I have to find her,' Daniel said.

Korel put the tray down on the bed and moved over to the window.

'That street leads down to the port this way,' she said,

indicating with her hand, 'and that way leads towards the hills behind the town. You came down from the hills, right? Well, I would check towards the port first.'

'Thank you, you truly are a godsend,' Daniel said with a faint smile.

Korel laughed. 'I don't know about that, but thank you for the compliment. And please, call me Korel. Now, go find her, and take these with you.'

She wrapped some sandwiches in a metallic cover taken from her apron pocket and handed them to Daniel.

He thanked her again, sliding them into his pocket.

Pushing the window fully open, he climbed through and jumped down to the dirt street below. The white disc of a full moon broke through passing clouds. Looking at Altinor's moon always made Daniel think of Earth, and whatever other worlds were out there, beyond the Solar System. But Earth most of all.

Making for the port the way Korel had shown him, Daniel could see no sign of Kala. He had half-expected her to run off at some point, but hadn't thought she would take the jewel. He shouldn't have fallen asleep. It made sense, she missed her mother; but he missed his, too, and *she* was alive.

He walked farther down the street, feeling uncomfortable in the rather baggy jumper Korel had given him before he left. It was warm, at least. He crossed paths with a few people at a junction hauling carts filled with fresh fish. The smell was strong, whetting his appetite. His mother often cooked salmon with baby potatoes and green beans for dinner. He used to soak the salmon in lemon juice so it looked like it was floating in the sea. He munched on one of the sandwiches Korel had given him.

A dog barked from a nearby doorway. He would search the whole town and beyond to find the jewel.

It wasn't long before he reached the port, still bustling with fishing boats passing in and out beneath Altinor's moonlit sky. Sunburnt men were pouring hundreds of different kinds of fish, some of which looked very alien to Daniel, onto the stone quayside between thick metal moorings. He looked along each side of the port. No sign of Kala. Seeing a horse drinking from a trough in the distance, he decided to go and ask its owner if he had seen her. Perhaps they might even help him find her.

Despite the full moon making the horse's true colouring hard to establish at first, the horse reminded him of Alpona. As he approached, Daniel could make out a man in what could best be described as a worn hooded poncho speckled with green and brown, talking to some fishermen. He looked familiar. It couldn't be ... It was!

Ketch spotted him, spoke a few more words to the men and then walked over, grinning.

'See you made it here in one piece!' Ketch said.

'And *you* made it too! I can't believe it! Is that you,

Alpona?'

'Don't you recognise me, Daniel?' the horse spoke, showing off her yellow teeth.

'How did you get here so fast? Alpona, how did you escape the Delvidrans?'

'Lokash saved me. You know, the Phib guard with the gun? While I was a captive surrounded by Delvidran soldiers, and being marched over a wooden bridge across the Dran river, he climbed under one of the bridge logs unseen and gave an almighty kick while I was crossing above him. I slipped and fell into the river with a couple of soldiers and a Radiant. I remember the disturbing sight of the person within the Radiant, still, seemingly lifeless, fuelling the machine. I can't get it out of my mind. The Delvidran captain's horse only just kept her balance. I wish the captain had fallen in the Dran, that would have been a sight for sore eyes! The current took us away from the bridge, and Lokash dropped into the water to follow us. The Radiant who fell in fizzed violently with electricity, short-circuited and sank beneath the surface. The river also took the soldiers down with their armour. The captain shouted, 'Kill the toad!' to the remaining Radiants on the bridge. Those hideous machines struck Lokash with terrible flashes of lightning, leaving his body bobbing on the water. It looked like lightning, but even though I was in the water, its electricity never reached me. Lokash's body gave off a horrible green steam, his skin bubbling and cracking. Oh, it

186

was the worst thing I have ever seen!'

'The captain will pay for this!' Daniel said.

'Lokash never shied away from a fight,' Ketch said. 'It was selfless and courageous of him. I think the Radiants' lightning didn't hit you too through the water because it is powered by biotricity from the poor souls within the machines fuelling them. Biotricity, gods help us, can be more targeted than electricity and water doesn't conduct it.'

'He may have been a pain in the backside most of the time, but he gave his life for me. I can't stop thinking about that,' Alpona said sadly.

If I hadn't met Alpona and Ketch and gone to Phibia and the Rusted Station, this would never have happened, thought Daniel.

'How did you both get here?' Daniel asked.

'When I managed to clamber out of the river,' Alpona said, 'I caught my breath on the bank for a while, then made for Jassk across the Savan Plains. It was a long gallop, but I knew that even though the chance of finding you both was slim in such a large city, I had to try. As I travelled across the plains, I saw in the sky above the city what looked like a falling star. It appeared to be dropping towards the east of Jassk, beyond the Beam Wall. When I reached the city's East Gate, mounted soldiers were rushing out, like they were on a mission. Merchants on horseback were heading in the same direction. There, on horseback, was Ketch. I thanked my ancestors for the coincidence and caught up with him. He said the falling star was in fact a plane.'

'Tarnat spotted the plane in the sky from the street where the hotel was. I looked at it through binoculars. It was definitely heading for a crash landing, but there was no obvious external damage,' Ketch said.

'How did you know I was on the plane?' Daniel asked.

'No planes have ever flown from Jassk before. In fact, ordinary citizens aren't allowed to use aircraft. I figured it must have been the consul's, or maybe the ministers'. As it was falling through the sky, I thought the pilot inside must be being prevented from flying the plane, or it must have been damaged internally. I didn't know for sure, but I had a hunch that you might have something to do with it. I knew I'd have to get to the plane to check before anyone else got there. Also, I would need to return quickly if you had died or were not amongst the wreckage, as the Jasskians would only turn off the Beam Wall for a few hours to enable their soldiers to investigate. I couldn't buy a horse with altins. Luckily, Tarnat knew someone who could lend me one. I told him and Niya to look out for your return at the Yavos Hotel if I was wrong. By even more luck, Alpona arrived at the East Gate at the same time. I knew that once she had let me on her back we would overtake all of the other horses.'

'The merchants on horseback were trying to beat the soldiers to salvage whatever they could from the wreckage,'

188

Alpona explained. 'Apparently, some bizarre Jasskian law allows whomever reaches something first that crashes in Jassk's surrounding lands to claim it as theirs, such as chunks from a meteor, and other rare impacts like that.'

'A bit like finders keepers?' Daniel said.

'What?' Alpona said.

'Never mind. You were saying?'

'Jassk treats the Cadaveri Desert beyond the Beam Wall as part of its lands, even though this is disputed by the people who live there. As Ketch said, I let him on my back and galloped towards the Beam Wall. When we got there, its beam had already been switched off. I doubt they wanted those living beyond the Wall to get their hands on any of the plane's parts. I reached the wreckage first. The soldiers and merchants were far behind. After realising you weren't there, we thought it best to return to Jassk, but Ketch spotted two sets of children's footprints. We followed them farther into the desert, but they became faint due to the Cadaveri winds. So we travelled here across the sand, stopping at any oasis or well we could find, hoping you were one of the owners of the footprints and that you had made it to Forjan.'

'Well, I'm relieved you are both here, Alpona.' Daniel smiled. 'Before I climbed into the consul's palace to search for the jewel, I agreed with Ketch to rescue you as soon as I'd found it and left the palace.'

'Don't worry, boy. I know finding the machine parts is of

paramount importance. You will note that I have come bearing no ill feelings. I'm here to ensure that you don't make a complete fool of yourself during the rest of the journey,' Alpona whinnied.

'That's the Alpona I know!' Daniel laughed.

'And the one I've suffered for much longer,' joked Ketch.

Alpona narrowed her eyes at Ketch and snorted.

'Still have the rubber belt, I see,' Ketch said with happiness in his voice. 'Did you find the jewel?'

'I did,' Daniel said, 'but a girl tried to stop me taking it and got locked in the same plane I escaped in.'

'You mean crashed!' Ketch grinned.

Daniel grinned back in embarrassment.

'So where is she now?'

'In the town somewhere. Or possibly even beyond it by now. While I was asleep in a room at an inn, she took the backpack with the jewel inside and disappeared. We have to find her!'

'Well, we can do a sweep of the town with Alpona's assistance,' said Ketch. 'The girl may be hiding somewhere. The platoon of Jasskian soldiers that were behind us will follow what tracks remain, and might make the connection and head here, since this is the nearest settlement to the crash site. We don't have much time. We'll have to check every street and inn in town. Someone may be harbouring her, so we can't trust anyone.'

Chapter 14

AYELET

Ketch and Daniel rode Alpona around the town, searching. If he ever managed to recover the jewel and find the remaining machine part—the main box of the generator—he remembered that the portal could be used by anyone. Despite all that they had been through together, he was still uncertain of Ketch's motives. While they looked for Kala, they discussed how she and Daniel had crossed the Cadaveri Desert and the moment the Beam Wall had been turned off temporarily. Ketch asked if he still had everything he needed to load the flintlock. Daniel told him how he had used his powder flask to store water. Ketch ensured Daniel's powder flask was dry and poured around half the powder left in his own flask into Daniel's.

Retracing his steps to the window of the inn that Kala had left open, they found no clues. So they searched the streets near the cliffs behind Forjan. They rode Alpona around Forjan for hours and hours until the sun began to rise over the horizon. Ketch asked people if they had seen her, but no one had. Alpona said her hooves were now very tired.

Daniel suggested they go back to look for clues at the inn in the main square where he had last seen Kala. When they arrived, the bustle of the inn was spilling out onto the square, and clusters of people, some drunk, some happy, some sad, thronged outside its entrance. Sharp rays of dawn shot through the streets adjacent to the square, causing them to squint. Ketch put on his sunglasses, and fitted Alpona's. Daniel looked through the crowds and thought he saw a glimmer of red hair between the bustling bodies. He and Ketch dismounted Alpona so as not to attract attention.

'Come on,' Daniel said.

'My hooves are killing me,' Alpona moaned.

'I think I saw her.'

'Let's go then,' Ketch said.

As they neared the people outside the inn, some complimented Ketch on his horse and offered Alpona a drink from their hip flasks. Alpona nickered out of politeness, but did not wish to encourage them.

'Drunken ignoramuses,' she said when they were out of earshot, 'thinking I'm *anyone's* horse.'

Suddenly, fifty feet or so in front of them, Daniel spotted Kala talking to a smiling but rather unsteady old couple hugging each other, as much for balance it seemed as for affection.

'There she is!' Daniel shouted.

The man and woman shook their heads and Kala turned. She spoke a few more words to the couple and then walked away.

'Quick, she's seen us!' Daniel said.

They began to head past the crowds and down the street Kala had taken. Kala began to run, dashing into a side street off the square, the backpack bobbing up and down on her shoulder. Alpona told Daniel and Ketch to get on her back, and they jumped on. When they were thirty feet away from Kala, she stopped. A group of men coming down the narrow street blocked her way.

'Where you going in such a hurry, sweetheart?' one asked.

'What's this?' asked another, pulling the backpack from her shoulder.

Daniel looked at the four men. He could see green light shining from digits on the uncovered right wrists of two of them. They made him think of Mark and his stupid friends at school, who bullied him and his mates. He knew what it was like to be outnumbered. To feel helpless. Daniel took the flintlock from his belt.

'Give that back! Don't you touch me,' Kala cried, whipping out a cutlery knife she must have stolen from the inn.

'Ha-ha, you think that's gonna stop Larkon Modner?' said the one who had spoken first.

'From her accent, sounds like she's not from here; Jassk maybe,' said another.

'Give me a peck on the cheek, love,' the first one said.

193

Avoiding her knife, the third and fourth members of the group grabbed her arms and legs respectively while she shouted and struggled, letting go of the knife. Daniel raised the flintlock. Ketch snapped a pistol from his own belt and aimed it at Daniel before the boy had even finished raising his. Daniel cocked the weapon and looked Ketch in the eye.

'What are you up to?' Ketch said.

'Trust me!' Daniel exclaimed.

With Ketch's pistol still trained on Daniel, Daniel aimed at the man with the backpack.

'Drop the backpack. Now!'

The group paused. Then the thug with the backpack began to laugh.

'Or what? You going to shoot me, boy?'

'Drop it or I will put a bullet in your brain. I'd say it would be an improvement.'

Still grinning like a fool, the man let go of the bag.

'Now take a few steps back.'

The man did not move.

'You're not going to get away with this. You don't cross us. No one's stupid enough to threaten the Modner Gang.'

'I won't tell you again,' Daniel said.

The man stepped back, and with his gun still trained on the target, Daniel picked up the backpack from the dusty street and checked its contents. The jewel was still there. He drew the strings of the bag tight before placing it on his back.

The two men holding Kala, one of whom was wearing a cowboy hat, turned and started to move away. Alpona aimed her leg at the third man, kicking back a hoof to scare him. He backed away, too.

'Stop!' Daniel shouted, aiming his gun at one of the two men carrying Kala.

'You can't have her too, you greedy runt!' said the thug holding her legs.

'Let her go!'

'No chance, boy,' said the other.

A loud crack rang out that made everyone jump. Daniel looked over at Ketch, his smoking gun still in the firing position. The bullet had left a hole in the top of the cowboy hat. Removing his punctured hat, the thug's legs started to shake, causing him to fall to his knees, loosening his grip on Kala.

'Do what he says,' Ketch said.

'You'll live to regret that,' the man said.

Ketch drew a second pistol and aimed at the men. With a smirk of admiration, he passed Daniel a bullet, which he loaded into the barrel; then he primed and cocked the gun. The gang began backing up slowly, still holding Kala. The one who had carried the backpack glared at Daniel.

'Wasn't even loaded!' the thug sighed.

'Let her go or the next bullet will be through flesh,' Ketch threatened. '*No*? Daniel, would you do the honours?'

195

Daniel shifted. He had never wanted to kill anyone. He remembered the soldier at Jassk's train station. That was self-defence. He took aim to injure, not to kill.

'Wait!' their targets said in unison, dropping Kala onto the street.

'Now run, or the mayor will be informed of this,' Ketch said.

'We're not afraid of that old bird!' the first one croaked.

The gang nonetheless fled, shouting expletives. Daniel went over to Kala to help her up. She patted away his hand and got to her feet.

'Are you all right?' he asked, concerned. 'This is Ketch, and that's Alpona.'

'I was okay until *you* found me! Look what you got me into!'

'What *I* got you into? If you hadn't run off with the jewel ...' He glanced at Ketch and Alpona. 'I don't want to argue.'

'For the last machine part to create the portal, we have to find Ayelet Szor, the scientist,' Ketch said.

'Portal?' Kala said. 'Don't tell me you're mad, too?' She cocked her head, indicating towards Daniel.

'I'm sorry to disappoint you,' Ketch said playfully, 'but concerning the portal, yes, it is possible to create one with the right machine.'

'A portal to where?'

'Well, anywhere you know the coordinates for, but in

this wretch's case, a world called Earth.'

'Wretch?! Pot calling the kettle black,' Daniel said.

'Anyway, let's get moving,' Ketch said. 'We'll try that inn you stayed at first; someone must know something about Ayelet.'

When they arrived back at the square, many of the night revellers had gone home.

As he entered the inn again, Daniel could see beer spills and the occasional piece of broken furniture—all that was left of a busy night. Korel was cleaning the floor while Jhor moved around the tables and chairs, wiping surfaces and collecting glasses. One skeletal old man crept past the group and made for the bar.

'Time, Telic! We're closed!' Korel growled at the man, who was teetering while stationary.

She looked at Jhor, who turned the old man round, put a huge arm over his shoulders—more in a headlock than a hug—and marched him to the door. Once released, the man walked in a zigzag line towards the light of the square.

'You lot, too!' Jhor bellowed.

'We're not here for a drink!' Kala said.

'We are here to ask your advice,' Ketch said.

Jhor stopped wiping tables and Korel looked up from cleaning the tired-looking carpets.

'Ah, sweetie, you're back!' Korel said to Kala. 'Your friend and I were worried about you.'

'Is that a *horse*? It can't be in here,' Korel said.

Alpona looked at Daniel.

'Prejudice,' she said.

Jhor almost dropped the glasses he was holding.

'Wait a minute! You're a ... talking horse?!'

'Even worse! Get out!' Korel shouted.

Alpona huffed. 'To think the people of Altinor used to call us the Sacred,' she said to Daniel.

'Sacred?' Kala said.

'The one known tribe of horses that speak. The other horses of this continent do not share the same vocal cords,' she explained.

'I've read about you.' Kala smiled. 'Where is your tribe?'

Alpona did not have time to reply.

'Out!' Korel shouted. 'What do you want, and why do you keep company with a talking horse?'

'Let it go, Korel,' Jhor said; 'he's sacred.'

'*She*,' Alpona corrected.

'I don't care who the horse is, he's not coming in!' Korel roared.

'*She*,' Alpona repeated angrily.

'My name is Ketch and this indeed *sacred* horse is Alpona.'

'Nice to have some recognition every once in a while,' Alpona said sarcastically.

'Alpona, please wait outside,' Ketch said.

'You're taking *her* side? She's being ignorant and you know it!'

'I know,' Ketch said in a hushed tone, 'but we need to find Ayelet.'

'Arggh!' Alpona snorted, turning on her hooves with a swish of her tail. 'I don't want *her* help anyway.'

She trotted out of the door, and Daniel saw Korel give a sigh of relief.

'I gather you've met Kala and Daniel,' Ketch said. 'We travelled here from beyond the Beam Wall looking for a scientist by the name of Ayelet Szor.'

Jhor's expression changed to one of faint surprise.

'You're looking for *her*? She lives in a large ruin of a house down by the port. Shame, really. It's the only one with black shutters; you can't miss it. Don't know what you'll manage to get out of her, though. People say she rarely leaves the house now. She was once in here, must have been about a year ago, spouting numbers and nonsense. Thought she was drunk, so we didn't serve her a drop.'

'Didn't seem to stop you serving most of your clientele last night,' Kala said in a low voice to Ketch.

Ketch thanked Jhor.

'Thank you and Korel so much,' Kala said. 'I don't know what I would have done without your help.'

'Yes, thank you both for everything you've done,' Daniel said.

'Don't mention it,' Korel said. 'We know you would do the same for us.'

'I'd be careful passing through town if I were you,' Jhor said. 'I don't think the people of Forjan have heard accents like yours for a long time ... if ever. In particular, I'd be careful talking with that horse in public.'

'We shall bear that in mind, thank you, sir,' Ketch said.

As they left the inn for the port, Daniel noticed Ketch had a more purposeful stride.

The house with the black shutters was easy to find. Cutting an imposing shape on a wooden pier to the right of the main quay, the building, lonely and forbidding, loomed above the bay. Scarred by the ravages of time and lack of maintenance, Daniel imagined it was once the proud home of a fishing magnate or whaling tycoon. He leapt past Ketch up the front steps and knocked firmly on the door three times.

The door creaked open, but there was no response from inside. They walked through the great hallway, the wooden floorboards groaning underfoot. Windows in a cluttered living room were open, the long drapes fluttering in the breeze. At the centre of the far wall stood a large fireplace, its grate filled with grey ash and the black remains of burnt wood. It looked like it hadn't been used in a long time. A dusty wooden bookshelf full of thick tomes and maps reached the ceiling on the right wall.

Ketch started to head up the stairs in the hall to the next

floor when a loud thumping sound was heard farther up.

'Ayelet,' Ketch said.

Daniel could make out a long silhouette on a wall on the landing above the stairs, tall, with long hair. Ketch moved slowly towards it and the others began to follow, except Alpona.

'I'll stay here, thank you very much,' she muttered.

Suddenly, the figure bolted down the stairs, barging past Ketch and the children before stopping in front of Alpona.

'Umm, guys?' Alpona gulped.

The woman was looking Alpona straight in the eyes, breathing heavily. The light streaming in from the living room windows revealed a pale, gaunt face with green eyes gleaming through a thicket of bedraggled blonde hair.

'Ayelet!' Ketch said again, speeding down the stairs.

He placed an arm on her shoulder. She spun round and, with a strength that was surprising for her frail body, grabbed hold of Ketch and forced him back. She looked disturbed, as though a light within had gone out a long time ago.

'Modner! Modner! Out!' Ayelet screamed at Ketch.

'It's me, Ketch.'

'Modner! Don't laugh! Don't joke!'

Before anyone so much as moved, she drew a short knife from within her tattered clothes and pressed it against Ketch's neck.

'We are not Modner, we are friends. Ayelet, it's me,

Ketch. Did they laugh at you?'

Daniel noticed that Ayelet had neither a currency storer nor a barcode on her wrists. Ayelet turned her head and stared at him.

'Time,' she mumbled.

A grandfather clock chimed. She lowered her knife and walked slowly towards him. Daniel took a few steps back, preparing to dart out of the way if the woman pounced on him.

'We need your help, Ayelet,' Ketch said.

Ayelet kept staring at Daniel.

'He is from Earth,' Ketch said.

She twitched.

'We are trying to help him return by looking for parts to make a stardeath generator,' he explained.

Moving between her and Daniel, Ketch put his hands on her shoulders.

'Ayelet, where is the box generator I gave you?'

Ayelet's stare broke and she looked at Ketch. Daniel caught his breath. The look in her eyes changed from fiery to frightened, and suddenly, she bolted for the door. *What had happened to her?* Something about the woman reminded Daniel of his aunt.

Ketch leapt between Ayelet and the door. She pushed and struggled to get past him, but Ketch talked softly to calm her down. Eventually, the pushing stopped, and, crying, she hugged Ketch tightly. After a minute or so, Ketch led the terrified woman by the hand back into the living room and convinced her to sit on an armchair by the dusty fireplace.

'I'm sorry to frighten you, Ayelet,' Ketch said. 'I swear they will pay the price.'

Ayelet stared at the billowing curtains. With his thumbs Ketch gently wiped the water from her cheeks. The woman stopped crying, her tears replaced by what Daniel thought was a fire in her eyes. *She even looks like Aunt Laura.* His aunt had suffered a breakdown when Uncle James was away with the army. They called it psychosis. He remembered going with her and Mum to pick up her medicine and take her to and from therapy. She recovered after being treated, thank god. She returned to being the aunt he knew.

'Shelf,' Ayelet said in a loud voice.

'Do you want something from the bookshelf?' Daniel asked.

'Shelf,' she repeated, and pointed.

Daniel followed her finger to a dusty set of maps on a lower shelf of the great bookcase.

He lifted one off the top of the pile. The title read: *Southeastern Shard and Kotorr.*

'This one?' he said, pointing the map's face towards Ayelet.

'No!' Ayelet screamed.

'Ok,' Daniel said softly, picking up the one below it, 'how

203

about this one?' *Itta, Arloth and the surrounding islands.*

'No, no. All below!'

'The one below?' Daniel said, taking the next map. *The Melithusan archipelago.*

'Huh,' Ayelet grunted in frustration. 'All below!'

'I think Ayelet means the map at the bottom, Daniel. I *think*. Not sure,' Kala said.

'All below. Got it. Is this the map?' Daniel said to Ayelet, pulling out the last one. *Eastern Shard and the Oargrind Sea.*

The woman looked at the map and nodded.

Daniel unfolded the map and laid it down flat on the table next to her armchair. Ayelet motioned to him to turn it over. A detailed set of smaller maps of towns was printed on the back.

While Ayelet was seated, Ketch moved the armchair so she was facing the table. She pointed to an island on the map of Forjan and the surrounding area, not far out from the bay.

'Is that where the box generator is? Are you sure?' Daniel asked.

'Dark!' Ayelet said.

'Excuse me?' Kala said.

'Dark!' the woman repeated, emphasising the spot on the map.

'We should go there when it's dark?' Alpona said.

Ayelet shook her head with some vigour.

'I don't understand, is that the name of the island?' Kala

204

said to Ayelet.

'No! Dark! Within. Dark!'

'Maybe she means a place on the island,' Daniel said.

'I think so,' Ketch said, 'Ayelet, do you mean a cave?'

'*Cave!* Cave, cave. Cave,' Ayelet nodded.

'The box generator is in a cave?' Daniel asked.

Ayelet nodded again, a nervous smile forming on her face.

'Why didn't you just say so?' Daniel laughed.

Kala rolled her eyes.

'When did you last use the box generator? Does it still work?' Ketch asked.

Ayelet looked at him, but gave no response.

'It should be okay,' Ketch said. 'So long as it isn't badly damaged I can probably fix it anyway. To reach Earth, we have to try to make a wormhole in space.'

'I suppose we'll be needing a ship,' Kala said.

'Ship? A rowboat or two, more like. Not all of us are the consul's daughter,' Ketch said.

Horrified, Kala opened her mouth but no sound came out.

'Come on, your secret is safe with us,' Alpona said.

'How did you ...?' Kala stopped and looked at Daniel, who shook his head, and then at Ketch.

'Don't worry,' Ketch smiled, 'we'll get you back to your father, as long as you don't try to stop us finding the box generator. Ayelet, can you show me where the cave is on the island?'

Ayelet placed her finger on the map. Ketch grabbed a pen from a nearby writing desk and marked the spot. Then he folded the map and put it in the inner pocket of his jacket.

'Thank you,' he said.

Ayelet sat in silence, staring into space as if transfixed by something across the room.

'8 3 7 5!' she blurted out.

'What's that, Ayelet?' Kala said.

'3 7 5 8!' she shouted.

'What are those numbers?' Alpona asked.

'7 5 8 3!' Ayelet continued.

'One thing's for sure, they aren't coordinates,' Ketch said. 'It's okay, Ayelet.'

He put a reassuring hand on her shoulder. Her eyes met his and she let out a loud yelp, as though a bee had stung her.

'Next! Next! Next!' she shouted.

Ketch looked at the others.

'We'll go to the quay and see if we can barter with someone for a rowboat or two,' he said.

Daniel was not convinced. Was the story of the cave on the island true, or merely the ramblings of this poor woman? Was the box generator really there, or would it be a wasted trip? He peered through the tall windows at the endless grey sea. As the others said their goodbyes, he lingered in the living room, watching Ketch take Ayelet's shaking hand and crouch in front of her.

'I'm so sorry for what they did to you, and for bursting in like this. I promise I'll come back for you, my friend ...'

Letting go of her hand, he turned and left the room after Daniel, and joined the others waiting outside.

Chapter 15

BEYOND THE BAY

After much haggling, Ketch managed to buy two rowboats from fishermen in the port, and they were casting off for the island that Ayelet had shown them on the map. Daniel found it odd that after all this time avoiding using his currency storer to pay for things, as the transactions would be traced, Ketch would pay for the rowboats with his altins. When Daniel asked him about it, Ketch said that he had had no choice. The fishermen would only sell the rowboats, not lease them, and would only accept altins; no one in Forjan would accept anything else. No gifts. No bartering. He thought finding the third part of the portal generator outweighed the risks.

Daniel had never had good associations with the sea. Even at its most inviting, while at the beach in Spain on holiday with his mum and sister a few years ago, he never swam too far from the shore. Despite this, he had agreed to Ketch's idea for him and Kala to go in one boat and him to row, while Ketch and Alpona went in the other.

'I do not like the possibility of falling in the water and am really considering waiting for you at the port,' Alpona said, visibly shaking.

'Oh come on, get in, you'll be all right,' Ketch said.

Kala took a seat on a thwart near the front of the rowboat. Daniel gripped the rubber belt that lay across his shoulder, stepped into the rowboat, sat down on the rower's thwart and put the backpack underneath.

'I never imagined being on the Oargrind Sea,' Kala said. 'Any sea, for that matter. It's one I've read about many times, but never thought I would actually see.'

Kala jumped as Alpona dropped into the other rowboat next to them, her hooves rocking the craft.

'Calm down, Alpona,' Daniel said. 'You don't want to sink before you get there.'

Alpona's eyes narrowed. 'What are you saying about my weight, titch?'

'Nothing! You're so sensitive lately.' Daniel smiled.

'Alpona has always been sensitive. Come on,' Ketch said, patting her shoulder, 'you can do this.'

'Do what? Leave port in these little boats while the waves grow larger?' Kala said. 'If you're nervous Alpona, then at least I'm not the only one.'

Ketch undid the other rowboat's ropes and lifted its oars into place on the rowlocks.

'As a filly, Alpona fell in the moat around Mornaren Castle,' he said with a half-smile.

'Ah, so *you* fell in the moat too,' Daniel said.

'You didn't have to *tell* them,' Alpona squealed, her ears

209

pinned back against her head. 'I'm going to have to try to balance the whole way there,' she huffed. 'Being a horse has its drawbacks. Rarely, but on this occasion.'

'We'll go slowly,' Ketch said. 'Try to wrap a hoof under a thwart.'

'How far is the island?' Kala said.

'Not far, according to the map,' Ketch said. 'We'll need to find the box generator today. As I mentioned, Delvidran and Jasskian soldiers passed the Beam Wall after us. If we don't locate it soon, I fear we'll not have the chance later.'

'Here's hoping we find the cave today then!' Kala said.

While Ketch pushed his boat away from the dock with an oar, Daniel felt a cold breeze on his face. The wind was picking up, and the ripples that had lapped the sides of the boat moments before had given way to stronger, slapping waves.

'I suppose you should know I'm actually grateful to you for saving me from the gang of thieves in the town,' Kala said. 'I know it may not seem like my priority, but I want you to get home.'

Daniel gave her a faint smile.

'Help me get the boat moving,' he said.

Kala undid the mooring rope from the cleat on the quay while Daniel placed the oars in their rowlocks. He wondered how soon her father would find them. Or the Delvidran captain. It was only a matter of time. His thoughts drifted to his own father, of whom he had no memory, since he was only a toddler when he left.

He lifted an oar and pushed the rowboat away from the dock. Kala sat quietly on one of the thwarts in front of him. She looked nervous. His eyes shifted to Alpona, who teetered on each hoof, trying to keep her balance as Ketch began to row away from the dock. Alpona tilted her head and looked back at him.

'This reminds me of the moat,' she shouted.

'Yeah,' Daniel agreed.

'Follow us,' Ketch shouted.

Daniel worked the oars with some difficulty, correcting the boat's direction through the swelling surf. Following the other boat, he rowed through the harbour, busy with vessels of different sizes, most of them fishing boats. When they were farther out in the bay, an enormous three-masted ship came into view. It turned into the harbour, causing their rowboats to bob violently in its wake.

'Bloody ship!' Daniel said, struggling to keep his oars in their rowlocks.

'I recognise that ship's flag from somewhere ...' Kala said.

Rounding a long rocky headland that jutted out into the sea to one side of the port, Daniel could see the sheer cliffs of a small island. Ketch waved to them and pointed towards it. Daniel could hear a loud rumbling in the dark grey clouds above.

'Let's hope the wind doesn't get any stronger,' Kala said, dipping her hand into the cold sea.

Daniel estimated that Ketch and Alpona's boat was no more than thirty feet ahead of theirs. They circled the island, looking for a place to disembark. Eventually, they found a narrow sandy beach lined with trees like mangroves on the far side of the island, beyond which a green hill rose towards the sky.

'That's steep,' Daniel said, pointing to the hill.

'Steeper than the bowsprit of any galleon I've read about,' Kala said.

Ketch leapt into the water, which came up to his knees, and began to drag the other rowboat onto the beach. While pulling the rope attached to the bow, he implored Alpona to do the same to make the operation easier, but she was not budging. He grabbed the backpack, jumped into the black waves and, stumbling where the shallow seabed was uneven, pulled his rowboat onto the shore, securing it by tying the rope around the trunk of a tree. Then he and Kala went to help Ketch.

'Get out, now! You'll barely get a hoof wet, *Your Majesty*,' Ketch said sarcastically.

'Keep your hair on, *oh wise one*,' Alpona retorted.

She looked at Daniel as she dropped down into the shallow waters, wincing as the waves pushed the water higher up her legs. Daniel and Kala joined the mooring rope Ketch was pulling and dragged the boat onto the beach.

'I'm not *that* heavy,' Alpona said. 'I also had a recent episode with water. The River Dran. Remember I told you? I almost drowned.'

'Well, in case you haven't noticed, you're on dry land, so shut up about it,' Ketch said.

He fastened the rope to another short tree with many roots exposed above the sand.

Alpona whinnied loudly. 'You're not the boss of me, Woodsman,' she said. 'I won't shut up, and you would do well to remember I am one of the Sacred.'

'One bit of recognition and you become all high and mighty. Some of us are actually trying to achieve something here. The Sacred is basically just a name given by people who don't really know what pains in the arse talking horses are.'

Alpona flicked her tail. Her eyes narrowed. Ears back.

'Well, *you're* the idiot who created guns! *You* messed up the entire planet by letting people like the Delvidran captain steal your blueprints and re-programme your robot. What a fool! So don't lecture *me* about being a pain in the arse!'

'If you blame me so much, why don't you do something about it?'

'Ketch, Alpona,' Daniel said.

'It's okay, Daniel,' Ketch said.

'No, it's not okay!' Daniel shouted. 'You're both acting like my little sister. I'm surprised you can't control yourselves

213

over one boat crossing.'

Ketch and Alpona looked at him with disbelief for a moment.

'Listen, Daniel, Alpona and I have been friends for many years. We argue sometimes,' Ketch said.

'You would say that, though I suppose there is no point arguing,' Alpona said, rolling her eyes.

'Okay, let's go!' Kala said. 'We want to find this cave before a storm comes.'

They walked along the beach, the verdant cliffs rising above them. The 'X' that Ketch had marked on Ayelet's map showed the cave to be on the northern tip of the island. The land narrowed between the cliffs and the sea, barely wide enough for Alpona to walk along. Moving in single file, they scoured the rock face for the cave. Daniel had estimated during the crossing from the mainland that the island was no more than half a mile long, and they had soon walked around it in a circle. Back at the beach, they stopped at the rowboats.

'Maybe Ayelet showed us something on the map that she and the rest of us wished was real, but actually doesn't exist,' Daniel said.

'No, it's here, I know it,' Ketch said, peering at the map.

The darkening clouds above them still refused to break, though gusts of wind shook the leaves of the trees by the beach, making an eerie, lonely sound.

'We haven't checked the top of the cliffs,' Kala said.

'Perhaps she meant the entrance is on the cliff edge, rather than in the rock face. Come on!'

She began to walk towards the steep slope behind the trees.

'It's worth a try,' Daniel said.

When they got to the top of the hill, they agreed to split up to cover more area. Daniel's eyes darted across the grass, searching for clues. Mum and Rachel were on his mind. His aunt and uncle too. *If we could just find this last piece of the generator and get the portal to work*, he thought.

Suddenly, he heard a dull clang of metal being struck.

'Oww! Hey, I think I've found something!' Kala shouted, holding her foot.

She had stumbled over what looked like a metal handle rising up from the ground. Daniel tried it, then Ketch, then both of them together. Kala joined them, but the handle still did not budge.

'Help me dig,' Ketch said, pushing his hands into the grass around the handle.

Daniel and Kala got on their knees next to Ketch and started digging; despite their best efforts, it proved almost impossible.

'Seems like Ayelet hasn't been here for a while,' Ketch said.

'Step aside for a moment, let me have a go,' Alpona suggested.

She turned round so that her back legs were touching the spot, and scraped the ground hard with her hooves. Great clumps of dirt flew up, causing more clangs and revealing more metal. Some strange clicking sounds came from beneath the surface.

'It's working! Alpona, keep going!' Ketch said excitedly.

Moments later, they were standing over a large square metal hatch. Alpona stopped digging and Ketch pulled away any remaining clumps of grass and dirt to reveal the edge. Near the handle were four metal rotating discs, each revealing the numbers zero through to nine.

'Looks like we need the combination,' Daniel sighed. 'Is nothing ever easy here?'

'Nothing worthwhile,' Ketch said.

'I'm not going to be able to fit in there,' Alpona said.

'Wait, didn't Ayelet say some numbers after she showed Ketch the island on the map?' Kala said.

'That's right!' said Ketch. 'The first four numbers were 8 3 7 5, if my memory serves me correctly.'

He turned the metal rollers. After putting in the numbers, he tried the handle. It didn't budge.

'I think 3 7 5 8 were the next numbers,' Alpona said.

They didn't work either.

'The last numbers she said were 7 5 8 3,' Ketch said.

Nothing. Daniel's face dropped.

'Looks like we'll have to go back to Ayelet and see if she

can tell us the combination,' Ketch said.

'Maybe it's a sequence,' Kala said. 'Ketch, after you told her to stop, she kept on saying *next, next,* remember?'

'So what do the numbers have in common?' Daniel said.

'Well, let's see ... anyone have a bit of paper and a pen?' Kala asked.

'Afraid not,' Alpona joked.

'Okay, what were the numbers again?' Daniel asked.

'She might have just been shouting random numbers,' Alpona said.

'8 3 7 5, 3 7 5 8 and 7 5 8 3,' Ketch said, ignoring her.

Daniel said the three sequences of numbers over and over to himself.

'Let's write them in the sand on the beach,' he suggested.

At Daniel's request, Alpona let him ride on her back to the beach. Kala asked even more politely, so Alpona carried the two of them down the steep hill. Ketch jogged alongside until Alpona sped ahead once the hill met the grassy flats. By the time Ketch had caught up with them, Daniel and Kala had dismounted, and Daniel was drawing in the sand with a thin branch he had found.

'The three sequences of numbers each have the same numbers in them, but in a different order,' he said, peering at the numbers he had written in the sand, one sequence below the other.

'And look,' Kala said, 'the second sequence, 3 7 5 8, starts

217

with the second number of the first sequence, 8 3 7 5, which is 3, and continues with the 7 5 order, ending with the first number of the first sequence, 8.'

'8 3 7 5 becomes 3 7 5 8,' Daniel said.

'So they loop round,' Alpona said.

'Then 3 7 5 8 becomes 7 5 8 3, the third sequence,' Ketch said, breathing heavily. 'It starts with the second number of the second sequence, 7, and ends with the first number of the second sequence, 3.'

'So looking at the third sequence, 7 5 8 3, the fourth sequence following that looping pattern would be 5 8 3 7,' Daniel said.

'It could be completely wrong,' Kala said.

'But it's worth a try!' Alpona said.

Rushing back up the hill, Alpona let Kala and Daniel off at the hatch. The two of them moved the metal rotating discs into place and they heard a deep, satisfying click. Ketch, panting after running up the hill, smiled as Kala and Daniel yanked the hatch's handle. It gave suddenly, sending them flying backwards onto the grass.

'She was trying to tell us the code!' Kala smiled as she brushed off her clothes.

'Thank you, Ayelet!' Daniel said.

They peered into the darkness of the opening. There was a ladder formed from metal rungs fastened into the rock on one side of the shaft. Amidst the blustery winds Daniel was sure he could feel a slight breeze coming up from the darkness.

'Right, what are we waiting for?' Ketch said. 'Let's go.'

'What about Alpona?' Daniel said.

'I'll keep a lookout until you get back.'

'We'll be back soon,' Ketch said.

'Good luck, Daniel; I hope you find what you are looking for,' Alpona said.

'If we do find the box generator, I'll be back to say goodbye to you first,' he promised.

Though he didn't think he would, he felt sad at the thought of saying goodbye. He had never even thought about it until now. Perhaps he had been wrong to be suspicious of Alpona and Ketch.

Ketch clambered into the hatch first, in case of any danger he said, then Kala. Daniel climbed into the shaft last. After less than a minute, his feet touched solid ground. The tunnel was dark and he could barely see the shapes of Kala and Ketch ahead of him. A speck of light came from the far end, but it did not help much in seeing where he was going. It was not long until the tunnel opened out into a large cave.

Ketch took something from a pouch on his belt. Striking it against the cave wall, it lit up with sparks and a loud crackle. He held the flare above his head, and through the red light Daniel saw a large, old-fashioned travel trunk. There was a small lock, but Ketch made short work of it using a small hammer produced from his jacket pocket.

The three of them lifted the lid. Inside was a square dull-black metal box. On its front panel were buttons and levers, and on one side two metal spokes. Daniel didn't think it looked anything special, but he knew this was the last part of the portal machine.

'That's it! The box generator,' Ketch said. 'We now have the three parts of the machine needed to create the portal. What do you want to do now, Daniel? It is your decision.'

Daniel touched the rubber belt on his shoulder. Gripping one of the backpack straps he looked at Kala, then Ketch. Kala was smiling, Ketch was not. He picked up the box with both hands; it was lighter than he had thought it would be.

'I want to say goodbye to Alpona before we see if this thing works. Then I would ask you to help send me back, Ketch.'

'Okay, back up top then,' he said.

When they reached the top of the ladder, Daniel placed the box on the ground next to the hatch and climbed out.

'Well, it seems you've found it. Daniel, I am so happy for you,' Alpona said. She bared her teeth in a grin, but there seemed to be something else, some other emotion in her eyes.

'I wanted to say thank you to you and Ketch,' Daniel said, 'for helping me all this way, and for believing in me when I didn't believe in myself. And you, Kala, I don't think I would have made it out of the desert or found the last piece of the machine without you. Ketch, Alpona, please make sure Kala gets the jewel back after I've gone through the portal and finds her father.'

'We promise, Daniel,' Alpona said.

'Ketch, please could you set up the machine and enter the coordinates for Earth? Preferably Closeburn, in Dumfriesshire, Scotland.'

He took the black rubber belt and backpack from his shoulders and raised them in his hands towards Ketch.

Suddenly, flashes of light came from the beach below. Radiants! Four of them. Their rowboats were on fire!

'Open the portal!' Daniel shouted to Ketch.

'Drop what you have in your hands. One move, Daniel, Kala, and I shall order the Radiants to fire on your acquaintances.'

It was the captain of the Delvidran Guard. King Ordran's right hand. How had she known where to find them? Daniel's heart was pounding in his chest and his breathing quickened. He looked at Ketch and Alpona, then let go of the rubber belt and backpack. He had been so close to going home ...

'Father!' Kala shouted.

The helmeted Delvidran captain and the rangy, dark-skinned consul were both on horseback, advancing up the hill towards them. Delvidran and Jasskian troops fanned out from large rowboats on the beach. The soldiers marched up the steep hill behind their leaders in two wide columns, one behind the other; the grey-clad Delvidrans were to the leaders' right, with the four Radiants forming their front line, and the dark-blue-armoured Jasskians were to their left. The Jasskian troops were marching in four rows. The Delvidran soldiers looked at least double Jassk's numbers. Daniel wondered if he could try to reach for his flintlock. He looked at Ketch; he was scanning the troops. *Better not this time,* he thought.

As they drew near, the captain's large blood bay horse snorted loudly. Wearing her usual black-plumed helm, her sword on her belt, the captain looked down at Daniel from the saddle.

'Here you are,' she said, her face cold and expressionless.

'Kala, come here!' the consul said as his horse pulled up alongside the captain's. His hair was close-cropped and dark brown, unlike his daughter's fiery red locks.

Kala hesitated. Her eyes became glassy as they filled with tears.

'Kala, get away from them. If they hurt you ... I swear I will kill them myself!' her father shouted.

As Kala walked towards him, he jumped from the saddle and hugged her tightly.

'They didn't hurt me, father, they're my friends! Don't let her take them,' she pleaded.

'How did you find us?' Daniel asked the captain.

'Your friend's altin transaction for the rowboats was

picked up in Jassk. The consul was told via his radio communicator by Jassk's council of ministers the exact location where the purchase was made. We guessed that Ketch would have no need for a second rowboat if he was alone.'

'Look what you've done, Ketch! Look what you've done!' Daniel said. 'It's like you wanted us to be found!'

'Daniel, listen to me,' Ketch said, 'I swear I had no choice. The fishermen would only accept altin payments. I hoped we'd find the box generator, send you home and escape this lot before they got here, but they arrived a little sooner than I hoped.'

The captain smiled. 'When we arrived, the Jasskians asked around at the port while I talked to your pitiful friend Ayelet Szor. I assumed you would go to her, as she researched portals. The woman was in no condition to tell us anything, so I thought if we used a few methods to encourage her ...'

'You tortured her?' said Ketch. 'I'll kill you for this!'

'Not if I kill you first!' The captain smirked. 'Ayelet Szor's body was deceptively strong the second time around, despite her mental state. She said nothing, only screamed, but I worked out where you were when she looked at the map of Forjan Bay that lay open on her desk. An island was marked on it. She died before we were finished with the interrogation.'

Ketch reached for one of the pistols, but was punched to

the ground and disarmed by an armoured Delvidran soldier.

'What the hell do you want with us anyway?' Daniel asked angrily, trying to hold back his tears.

'You are a fugitive from the king's justice. My troops and I are here to return you to the castle dungeon,' the captain said.

There was no hint of emotion in her eyes. Lifting her head, she continued.

'Alpona, you are also the king's prisoner. You eluded us once with the help of the Phib, who, as you know, is now dead, and Ketch, the king's former Collector, well, you are the not-so-unexpected icing on the cake. Lieutenant?'

'Yes, ma'am,' a swarthy, thick-necked soldier said, stepping forward.

'Put them in chains, and collect the items the boy dropped and the metal box.'

'No! Stop! He's just trying to get back to his family,' Kala cried, tears rolling down her cheeks.

Her father prevented her from running forwards.

The Delvidran lieutenant gestured to the soldiers in the second line behind the Radiants.

'Take them! Move it!'

Six moved forward. One Delvidran soldier took the backpack, the rubber belt and the box generator, while the others forced shackles on Daniel and Ketch. Daniel twitched with pain as the metal was tightened around his wrists. He

224

wondered if Alpona would try to make a run for it, but she stayed put, the presence of the Radiants no doubt discouraging such a thought. She reared above one soldier and kicked at another.

'If you do not come quietly, I shall have you executed on the spot,' the captain said. 'I am considering making you my new mount. I believe you are up to it, with some breaking in, but remember you are not really needed, Alpona.'

'You'll never ride me, I'll make sure of that!' she screamed, but stopped kicking.

The soldiers placed a heavy-looking bridle connected to a lead over her head and fastened it tight. She ground her teeth against the bit and roared at the soldiers.

'Now you have recovered your daughter and we have our prisoners, Consul, I would suggest we return to the boats and Forjan,' the captain said. 'As I mentioned, the king waits on the warship in the bay. He asks that you come to him to discuss a new treaty before your journey back to Jassk.'

'I shall speak with him, but only to clarify my view on the matter,' the consul said. 'Please, Captain, lead on to the beach.'

The captain dug her heels into her horse's flanks and began to descend the hill in the gap left between the Delvidran and Jasskian troops. The consul lifted Kala, her face wet with tears, onto his horse. He then joined her on its back.

Trotting over to Daniel, he said, 'My wife's jewel, hand it over.'

Daniel looked the consul in the eye for a few moments.

'In the backpack.' He sighed, pointing with his cuffed hands at the Delvidran soldier who was carrying it.

'You understand that as well as kidnapping my only child you destroyed my plane?' the consul said.

'I did not kidnap Kala!' Daniel shouted. 'She tried to stop me and followed me into the plane. Gave me a few scars, too. I only needed your wife's jewel to help me get back home to Earth.'

'And you never thought to ask?' the consul said.

He dug into the flanks of his horse and trotted on down the hill. Jasskian soldiers rounded the Delvidran soldier carrying the backpack. He hesitated, but then produced the large green jewel and lifted it up towards the consul. The consul leaned forward in his saddle, stretched out a hand beyond Kala and collected the jewel. Daniel, Ketch and Alpona walked at spearpoint to Delvidran boats. The troops rowed the boats across the sea to the port. The huge three-masted ship loomed above them in the bay. The name *Chorozon* was emblazoned on its stern.

Daniel felt sick to his stomach with anguish and anger. He would never be able to make it home to his mum and sister now. The king's soldiers and the consul had the machine parts, and finding the correct coordinates and instructions on how to use the portal generator from Ketch was all they needed to travel to Earth. The captain asked the consul to leave his horse with those of his bodyguards already at the quayside and some of his soldiers to tend to them. It appeared that if he did not, there would be no negotiation with the king. The consul replied there were guards already left in port tending to his troops' mounts, so he ordered but two guards ashore with his horse.

Once the two men had transferred with the consul's grey horse to a smaller boat and begun rowing to port, the remaining boats were positioned alongside the warship.

Daniel, Ketch and Alpona were coaxed with spears onto the deck of *Chorozon* and lined up side by side while the soldiers and ship's crew taunted them.

'Soldiers, ensure they kneel before the king,' the captain ordered.

The Delvidran soldiers forced Daniel and Ketch to their knees. Daniel struggled, but the soldiers pressed him to the deck. Alpona kept them away for longer, though eventually a group of them managed to get in close and heave her over. She lay on her side, kicking as they held her down.

'They haven't done anything!' Kala shouted.

The consul held her by the shoulders to prevent her from running to them.

Straining under a soldier's grip, Daniel looked up to see the man who had interrogated him from his throne in the castle emerge from elaborately carved doors at the ship's stern. The tall, self-obsessed man was clad from head to toe in white and gold armour, a sword in a jewel-encrusted scabbard at his side. The king smirked. Ketch looked up and matched his stare.

'The prisoners of Delvidran have been recovered,' the king said in a loud voice.

'Hoorah!' the soldiers and ship's crew shouted.

The king looked in the eyes of each member of the group. His face bore no emotion whatsoever.

'Take the traitors to the hold,' he ordered.

'They are not traitors; *you* are the traitor, to Delvidran!' Daniel said, a soldier's boot pressing down on his back.

The busy warship now seemed so silent, and Daniel felt more alone than he ever had in his life.

'Leave it, Daniel,' Ketch said. 'He will pay for what he has done to Delvidran and our world.'

'Silence, traitor!' the captain said. 'How dare you talk with our king before being spoken to? And who are you, boy? Perhaps you are lying and are from Altinor, some worthless whelp whose parents left him to rot in the desert of the Broken Waste.'

Daniel was about to reply when one of the guards sucker-punched him in the ribs.

'Captain,' the king barked, 'ensure that the prisoners remain in their cells until we arrive at the Port of Delvidran.'

'As you wish, sir,' she replied, smirking.

'No!' Kala screamed. 'You can't do this! Father, *please,* tell them!'

The king and a few soldiers left the main deck for the cabin. The captain ordered a guard to hold open the large hatch on the deck ahead of the main mast. As Daniel watched the soldiers force Ketch down into the bowels of the ship, he could hear Kala and her father talking loudly.

'Kala, the boy stole your mother's jewel from us,' the consul said. 'The man and the horse were his accomplices. They are prisoners of the king, and it is not for us to question why.'

'It *is.* Of course it is. Father, where did you lose your heart? The king wants a *boy* to be a prisoner. He *must* be asked why. You know the stories: this same king forced the wife of that man they captured to marry him and exiled the man. Alpona has done nothing wrong and is one of the few horses left that can talk. Many call them sacred, and knowing Alpona even for a short time I can see why. We must do something to help them!'

'I lost my heart when your mother died,' the consul said. 'Finding you again, at least I have part of it restored.'

Alpona managed to kick out at the guards behind her, but eventually, they forced her at spearpoint to follow the others below deck.

'Make sail for the Port of Delvidran,' the captain shouted

at the crew of the warship. 'Consul, you will follow me, please.'

The consul looked at his daughter and then took her hand, dragging her through the wooden doors to the king's cabin.

A strong hand gripped the back of Daniel's neck and another pushed him forwards, forcing him into the dark belly of the ship.

Chapter 16

CHOROZON

Daniel could see nothing but a small light from the porthole in the brig. Ketch and Alpona had been forced into the next two cells, but when they tried to talk, the guard told them to shut up and struck his spear on the metal bars. Daniel's chains were linked to the wooden floor of the hold through a metal loop in the centre of the cell. He moved as far as the chains allowed him and peered out of the porthole. White waves smashed against the side of the ship. The briny smell of the sea filled his nostrils and the sway of the ship made him feel sick. He took a few deep breaths, wondering how far they were from Forjan, or any port for that matter.

'Daniel, try to –'

Ketch began, but he was silenced.

'Which part of shut up do you not understand?' the guard shouted. 'From now on, if you make so much as a peep, I'll ask the captain if I can cut one of your ears off.'

Daniel thought about what Ketch had tried to say. Was there a way out of the chains and the cell? The guard banged the bars of his cell in the darkness. The noise made Daniel clasp his hands over his ears. Alpona squealed in pain.

'Don't think you'll get out of this one, boy.'

Daniel could see a glint of yellow from the guard's toothy smirk in the shaft of light coming from the porthole.

'Word is, you're to become a Radiant once His Majesty is done with you.'

'Why would he want to do that?' Daniel asked, not really expecting a reply.

'I don't know. I guess he wants you to serve him after death, too.'

Hope was fading fast.

'What about the others?' he asked.

'Word is, His Majesty and the captain have other plans for them.'

A shiver ran down his spine.

'If you tell His Highness and the captain the truth, they may put you in a coma painlessly. The Radiant armour will keep you alive and, in turn, will feed off your body until Delvidran no longer has a use for you. Cheer up, ha-ha!'

As the guard stomped off, Daniel slumped in a corner of the cell. The chance of him returning to his mum and sister now was very slim. Thoughts of what the king might do to Ketch and Alpona flooded his mind. He closed his eyes and tried to sleep, but the cold, damp hold and the noise of the crashing waves made it difficult.

Sleep would not come as the enormous warship rose and fell on the rough sea. Daniel spent several hours looking through the porthole until the sun had been replaced by moonlight and it began to rain. Lying on the wooden floor, he listened to the sound of Alpona snoring. How she could sleep at a time like this escaped him, but he was envious. The pounding noise outside became fainter and he looked out of the porthole. The rain had petered out, but the air felt much colder now. Daniel thought he heard a thud, then a voice. It was practically a whisper, but it seemed to be calling his name.

'Didn't think I'd leave without you lot, did you?' Kala said through the gloom.

Daniel could hear the jangling of keys and his despair turned into a flicker of joy.

'What took you so long?' he joked.

'Well, Daniel, I was a bit busy sneaking past the Delvidran soldiers. You should be grateful.'

'Kala! Oh, he's grateful, trust me,' Ketch said. 'We all know that he can be quite pig-headed sometimes.'

From the small circle of moonlight coming through the porthole, Daniel saw Kala open his cell door. She approached him, bent down and touched his arm while unlocking his chains.

'There you go.'

'Thank you,' Daniel said.

'There, that wasn't so hard, was it?' She grinned.

He stood up and smiled. As he followed her to the next cell, he stumbled like a drunk whenever the ship rocked. She freed Ketch and then Alpona, both thanking her profusely.

'How did you get past the guard?' Alpona asked Kala.

'I crept up behind him while he was sitting in the dark and hit him on the head with a wooden hammer I found in the forecastle; that's the sailor's quarters at the front of the ship.'

'You read too many books,' Daniel said.

'The jailer had the keys on his belt. Don't know how long he'll be out for, so we have to move quickly.'

Daniel noticed the green digits on Ketch's wrist now read twelve zeroes.

'They took the rest of your altins,' he said, pointing at Ketch's arm.

'The jailer stole them using a barcode reader,' Ketch explained.

'On deck there are more Delvidran soldiers than bodyguards my father brought with him,' Kala said. 'They overwhelmed the Jasskians and are guarding them. My father was captured by the king during negotiations in the king's cabin. He said he would keep us to demand a heavy ransom and favourable terms from Jassk's council. Before they could chain me I made a run for it and leapt through an open window at the back of the cabin. I tried to drag my father along with me, but I wasn't fast enough. As I got through the window and held onto the back of the ship, my father let go of my hand. I knew he did it to give me a chance. I could hear chains being put on him as he was held down by the Delvidran soldiers. I'm so worried. I wanted to help him! All I could do was try to find you. I climbed up the stern of the ship and edged along the outer side of the deck, all the while worried I would be seen. I lifted the lid of one of the gun ports and clambered past a cannon into the hull. Then I searched around in the darkness to find the brig. We have to free him!'

'We will, Kala, you can be sure of that,' Ketch said.

'Before we go creeping around we need to have a plan,' Daniel said. 'As Kala said, the deck is crawling with Delvidran soldiers and the king, and no doubt Kala's father will be well guarded.'

'We won't stand much of a chance with these hooves clomping about, however quietly I step,' Alpona said.

'If we can somehow free the Jasskian soldiers being guarded on deck, then we stand a chance,' Kala said. 'Alpona, if you guard the hatch to the deck, then Ketch and Daniel, you can come with me. We'll climb up the outside of the ship from some gun ports and find a way to distract the Delvidran soldiers.'

Alpona nodded her approval.

'You are more than the typical aristocrat's daughter.' Ketch smiled.

'How many aristocrat daughters have you met?' she replied.

'Too many,' he joked.

'Good luck,' Alpona said, baring her teeth. 'Let me know when it's all done.'

After searching near the guard's unconscious body, they recovered their belongings, including the flintlocks with their dry powder, wadding, flints and shot from a cupboard near the cells. Ketch and Daniel took time to load their flintlocks. A Delvidran soldier, on the command of the captain of the guard, had taken the rubber belt and the box generator on the island's hilltop. The consul had taken back the jewel needed to run the portal machine. Daniel knew it would take a lot more luck to get back home now, but it was still possible.

'If it rains again, tie this tightly around the pan when it's closed,' Ketch said, handing him an oiled rag. 'Should keep the powder dry.'

'Thanks; a real *hi-tech* idea,' Daniel said.

Ketch shot him a displeased look. Leaving Alpona on the gun deck, Daniel, Kala and Ketch each lifted a gun port lid on the ship's portside and made their way out past the cannons. Daniel took a deep breath. With the flintlock tucked into the back of his trousers, he climbed up the rigging on the outside of the ship. By the time they reached the edge of the deck, or gunwale as Kala whispered annoyingly, Daniel's arm and leg muscles were burning. They balanced on a thin wooden beam just below the edge, their hands still gripping the rigging. Ketch signalled with his hand for them to keep their heads below the edge while he peered over.

After a few seconds, he popped his head back down.

'The Jasskians aren't chained up,' he whispered, 'but they've put down their weapons and are being watched by Delvidran troops, a cluster in each corner of the deck. There are four Radiants, one stood in each corner beyond the soldiers. Alpona tells me they only act on the king's or captain's command, no one else's. A stroke of luck is that the captain is there, watching the deck, facing away from us. Now, if you follow me after a few seconds to back me up, I'll ambush her, and tell the Delvidran soldiers to free the Jasskians and bring the consul and the generator parts or I will kill her.'

Daniel was unconvinced. He knew first-hand about the captain's fighting skills.

'It's terribly risky,' Kala said in a hushed tone, 'but I guess if Daniel watches your back with his pistol we'll have a chance.'

'That's all we need.' Ketch grinned.

'I don't know if you've seen the captain fight. One false move and she'll beat you just as soon as you can say damn,' Daniel whispered.

'Damn?' Ketch said in a low voice.

'It doesn't matter,' Daniel whispered, drawing his pistol and bringing it up next to his chest. 'Let's do this.'

They pulled themselves up from the side of the ship and

jumped onto the deck. Ketch was a few steps ahead of Daniel and Kala, grabbed the captain from behind and pushed a loaded pistol to her chin.

'Move and I'll blow your brains across the deck,' he threatened.

'I'd recognise that stench anywhere,' she replied.

Kala moved forward a little and watched the troops ahead of Ketch and the captain. Daniel turned in the opposite direction to Ketch, aiming his flintlock at the nearest Delvidran soldier of a group guarding some Jasskian troops near the ship's many large rowboats.

'Listen up!' Ketch shouted.

The Delvidran and Jasskian troops looked up and froze.

'Unless you want your captain dead, bring me the consul and the machine parts.'

The Delvidran troops remained silent for a while, until one of the taller soldiers said, 'How did *you* get free? What machine parts?'

'Don't play dumb with me, boy,' Ketch said. 'The portable generator and rubber belt taken from us on the island. You have ten seconds.'

'Don't listen, men, he won't do it,' the captain said.

Daniel shifted nervously, but kept his gun on the closest Delvidran soldier behind Ketch and Kala.

'Ten, nine, eight, seven, six—'

'Okay, keep your knickers on, I'll tell the king,' the

Delvidran soldier said.

With his gun trained on the soldier, Daniel turned his head to see the mouthy soldier heading through the carved wooden doors of the cabin at the stern of the warship.

A few moments later, the doors flew open suddenly and the king strode out with his guards and the consul. The soldier who had informed the king of Ketch's demands had joined the ranks of soldiers guarding the king and his prisoner. His wrists chained, the consul looked tired, haggard even. Daniel wanted to help free him for Kala's sake, but he knew he had to get the jewel back. He turned to watch the Delvidrans behind Ketch and Kala.

'Why is this traitor free and threatening the captain of my Guard?' the king growled.

'I am no traitor,' Ketch said in a loud voice. 'Release the consul and bring the generator parts to me, and your captain will be spared.'

A cold silence ran through the deck like ice on Daniel's skin. After a while, the king spoke.

'Kill her. You cannot escape out on the ocean, traitor.'

Daniel craned his neck and looked at Ketch. He imagined Ketch was forgetting the Radiants at the corners of the deck. One word from the captain, and they could be fired at from four directions with bolts of energy. Why had he agreed to such a foolish idea?

In a blur, the captain let her legs fall to the deck. She

turned on Ketch, knocking the flintlock out of his hand and sending him flying with a roundhouse kick that Bruce Lee would have been proud of. The Delvidran soldiers facing Daniel edged forwards.

'Don't move!' Daniel shouted, his left arm shaking from the weight of the flintlock.

He looked around and watched as the captain pounced on Ketch, pressing a boot down on his chest.

'I am ready to die for my king, but today is not the day. And not at the hand of the likes of you,' the captain said.

She had a sword at her side, but instead drew a metal dagger with a long wavy blade from her belt.

'Today is *your* day, traitor,' she said as she grabbed Ketch's hair to scalp him.

'He's not a traitor!' Kala screamed. 'Alpona, now!'

With almighty force the flaps of the hatch door below the captain and Ketch erupted, propelling both of them into the air. A faint whinny rose from the ship's hold as Ketch and the captain came crashing down onto the deck.

Getting up and recovering her lost helmet, the red-haired captain placed it back on her head.

'Searcher! Kill this filth!' she shouted.

'Daniel! Look at the poop deck!' Kala yelled, pointing.

Daniel gave the nearest Delvidran soldier a grave look before turning back round. A familiar black shape rose from the deck above the cabin. *Another metal hawk*, thought

Daniel. It hovered for a moment before hurtling towards Ketch.

While all of the soldiers looked at the foul contraption, the Jasskian soldiers seized the moment and attacked their Delvidran captors. Daniel could see the king barking orders at some of his bodyguards and two of them dragged the consul back into the cabin. He ran to look inside one of the bulky rowboats on the main deck, where there were several sets of long, heavy-looking oars.

'You there, give me a hand with this!' he shouted to a Jasskian soldier nearby, who had seconds earlier knocked a Delvidran soldier unconscious with a well-timed right hook. Daniel pointed at one of the rowboat's oars. The Searcher was gaining on Ketch. The Jasskian soldier took one end of the oar and helped Daniel lift it out of the rowboat. While Ketch was about to dive over the edge of the deck, they heaved the oar between him and the Searcher, which was now feet from them. A small hatch on the flying hawk opened and a gun barrel came out.

Daniel let go of his end of the oar and shouted, 'Hit it!'

Zonn swung the heavy oar round, knocking the Searcher off-course. It flew off towards the moonlit sea, sputtering sparks and wisps of smoke. Ketch stopped running and turned round, out of breath.

'Thanks, what's your name?' Daniel said.

'Zonn,' said the soldier.

'My name's Daniel, and that's Ketch.'

'It's coming round again,' Zonn said.

The metal hawk corrected itself, making a wide turn over the sea and moving into position for another attack. With it accelerating directly towards them, Daniel and Ketch ran towards the ship's main mast, dodging clusters of fighting soldiers. Zonn swung again at the Searcher with the oar, but in vain. It scudded about three feet above the deck towards Ketch, and as Daniel dived out of the way he heard an enormous crash of metal. He looked back and saw the machine embedded in the wooden deck, broken and fizzing sparks. Going over to inspect the fallen metal hawk, Daniel saw two large round dents on its shiny body. Ketch was about three feet from it, a smoking pistol in each hand.

'Cheap knock-off,' Ketch said, mocking the captain's creation, now a downed bird of twisted metal and wires. He reloaded his flintlocks.

With the help of the Jasskian soldier and with the captain bearing down on them, sword in hand, Daniel and Ketch lifted up what was left of the wooden hatch flaps and helped Alpona clamber up onto the deck. While Zonn rushed forward to meet the captain's advance, Alpona gave out a long, eerie neigh and dashed around the deck, kicking any Delvidran soldiers stupid enough to stand and fight rather than getting out of the way. Ketch frantically tried to finish reloading, but after matching the Delvidran captain with each strike, Zonn fell to a swift, unexpected thrust to his side.

'No!' Daniel shouted.

He aimed his gun at the captain.

'You can't kill her in cold blood,' Ketch said. 'Death is too good for her. She deserves to be tried in Delvidran along with the king for they did to Ayelet, and Lokash, and the countless others they used to fuel their infernal Radiants.'

'They are but *one* of the ways I made Delvidran greater.' the captain said, her eyes flaring with anger under her helmet. 'Let me remind you of their power. Radiants One and Two! Kill this man, *without* damage to the ship.'

Ketch and Daniel ran across the deck between the main mast and the Delvidran bodyguards who were guarding the king from attacking the Jasskian soldiers. Daniel could see that the two Radiants in either corner of the bow end of the deck had begun to shake. Biotricity crackled loudly across their grim biomechanical bodies, charging up for a shot. The coma-induced people trapped within the machine's great armoured shells trembled as bolts coursed through their bodies, revealing their skeletons within intermittently. How the poor souls survived it, Daniel did not know.

Alpona knocked a soldier down who was trying to throw Kala into the dark sea. She let Kala mount her back and galloped up the steps to the stern deck to avoid great bursts of light that shot out from the Radiants' hulking metal bodies. Daniel and Ketch dived over the starboard side of the deck, clutching desperately at the outer rigging to stop themselves from plunging into the water below as two bolts shot across the edge of the deck, inches above their heads.

'That was close,' Ketch said, smiling.

'*Close?* A few seconds later and we would have been fried. I don't see how you can smile about it,' Daniel replied.

'*Because*,' Ketch said, while pulling himself up the rigging to the main deck, 'we've got them on the back foot.'

'How exactly?'

'Have a little faith, you'll see.'

Daniel climbed up the rope ladder and swung one leg, then the other, over the edge of the ship. He could see Alpona kicking at two Delvidran troops that had followed her to the stern deck. Kala was with her, hitting another Delvidran soldier on the head with a metal-ribbed wooden bucket while he loomed over an injured Jasskian soldier. Kala's attack caused the Delvidran to turn around, his eyes leaving his prey as he looked for Kala. This proved just the distraction for the Jasskian, who slit the Delvidran's throat with a dagger.

The king and the captain, whirling their swords around them, were leading the nine Delvidran soldiers that remained on the main deck against seven brave Jasskian soldiers. The Delvidrans had pushed the Jasskians back from in front of the cabin doors and towards the main mast. Daniel looked to each side of the mêlée at the corners of the main deck. The Radiants had settled, though they were tilting their enormous carcasses towards Alpona and Kala on the stern deck above. The people melded with them, motionless, their eyes closed; they did not know that the sole purpose of the machines was to kill and destroy. In fact, they seemed dead already. If each person within the machine exoskeleton was in a coma, and was ever freed and woke up, Daniel realised they would never know that they had taken part in all of these killings.

'How is this having them on the back foot?' he asked, concerned.

'We have time. Seconds, actually. Follow me. Alpona!' Ketch shouted.

Alpona pinned the last Delvidran soldier standing on the poop deck to the ship's wheel and pushed her weight forward, squeezing the breath out of him. Eventually, she took her hoof off his chest, and he collapsed in a heap. She then motioned for Kala to get on her back and they shot down the stairs to the main deck.

Daniel ran alongside Ketch to the centre of the deck. He did not like doing things without first knowing the plan. At that moment, the king threw a spear over the throng of fighting soldiers, which found its target. Ketch let out a cry and fell. Daniel saw that the spear was so deep in Ketch's right thigh that its metal point was no longer visible.

'No!' he cried.

They all rushed over to where Ketch lay, shielded from attack by the remaining Jasskian soldiers blocking the path to them with spear and sword. Daniel gripped the spear embedded in his friend's leg. Two other hands wrapped around the shaft, and with some difficulty, he and Kala managed to prise the spearhead out of Ketch's thigh. Ketch screamed in agony, banging the back of his head on the rough wooden deck beneath him.

Kala took out her makeshift bandana from the desert and tied it tightly around his oozing wound.

'Daniel, tear off the sleeves of your shirt,' she said.

Daniel did as requested and handed them to Kala, who tied them firmly over the reddening bandana.

'That should help with the bleeding,' she said.

'Thank you, Kala,' Ketch said hoarsely, smiling through the pain.

He turned to Daniel.

'No time to lose. Get the consul and the generator parts ...'

'We'll free your father, darling,' Alpona said to Kala.

Daniel checked his shot pouch. One bullet left and one in the gun. He did not have enough primer for the last bullet.

'Okay, Kala, you come with me,' he said. 'We'll get into the cabin through the windows in the stern, find your father and get the machine parts. Ketch, if you are still able to, cover us from the king's men till we're up those steps,' Daniel said, pointing towards the raised stern deck. 'We'll help you onto Alpona's back. Alpona, you keep Ketch away from the

246

Delvidrans and as soon as we're clear help the Jasskians. We'll meet at the rowboats.'

Kala nodded. Alpona snorted in agreement.

'Hey!' said Ketch, seeming surprised.

'What?' Daniel asked.

'That was almost as good as my plan.'

'Anything is better than your plans!' Daniel smiled.

Ketch laughed, adding to his pain. Daniel took one of his arms around his shoulder and began to help him up.

'Kala, give me a hand.'

Kala took Ketch's other arm over her shoulder and with some effort they managed to get him to his feet. He balanced himself on one leg and mounted Alpona's back painfully with their help.

'You all right?' Daniel asked him.

Ketch nodded, gripping Alpona's thick mane with one hand and lifting a flintlock in the other.

'Okay, let's go!' Daniel shouted.

'Radiants Three and Four!' the captain shouted after reducing the Jasskian soldiers from seven to six. 'Kill the man on the horse! Do not shoot anything else!'

Daniel ran for the steps to the poop deck at the ship's stern, with Kala not far behind him. Alpona galloped across the portside of the deck with Ketch, groggy, trying to stay on her back and keep his grip of a pistol. The Radiants at the bow end of the main deck charged up to fire, biotricity crackling across their metal shells. Fear shot through Daniel's body. A spear flew past about two feet ahead of him. He stopped for a second, but Kala pushed him on up the steps. Ketch loosed a shot, which felled a Delvidran soldier about to throw another spear at the children.

With no one else on the poop deck, at the top of the steps Daniel and Kala stole a quick look back. Alpona had carried Ketch to the front of the bow's raised forecastle deck opposite, out of the Radiants' line of fire.

'They can look after themselves, come on!' Daniel shouted.

Kala and him ran to the very back of the poop deck and slid over the edge, holding onto ledges and protruding parts of the ship's stern. They climbed a short way down until they were on a ledge above the large windows of the cabin. One of them had been left open.

'You lower me down and I'll look through,' Kala whispered.

'Why do I get all the hard jobs?' Daniel whispered back.

'Hard jobs? Are you joking? I'm lighter! Come on, hold my legs.'

Kala turned so that she was clinging onto the stern, flat on stomach, her head in the direction of the sea feet below them. She used her arms while upside down to pull herself level with the windows. Balancing on the ledge by using only his feet, Daniel struggled to keep a good grip on her trousered legs.

'Do not get seen! I can't hold you for much longer,' he whispered.

'Okay, up!' Kala said in a low voice.

Daniel pulled on her legs, straining with all the energy he could muster. Kala grabbed onto the ledge and turned back round while Daniel held her until she was upright and balancing on the ledge.

'I saw him!' she said. 'He's being guarded by two soldiers. They are all facing away from the windows, with my father in front of them.'

Daniel drew his gun, gripping the stern with his free hand.

'I'll go first,' he said.

They scrambled down the ship and through the open window as quietly as they could. Daniel aimed the pistol at one of the guards and cocked the hammer back. The guards and the consul turned round.

'One move and I'll drop you,' Daniel said, moving the gun barrel across from one guard to the other and then back.

'I disagree,' said the guard Daniel's gun was aimed at.

He took a step forward, lowering his spear to point towards Daniel. The other guard followed suit.

'You don't have the guts, boy,' the same guard said.

In a flash, Kala's father stepped forward and bashed the guards' heads together with his manacled hands. The two helmed soldiers dropped their spears and slid to the floor of the cabin.

'Thank you for providing a distraction,' the consul said.

'Daddy!' Kala shouted.

She ran over and hugged him.

'Sir, we have to get you off this ship,' Daniel said. 'We'll take you to the rowboats.'

'My wife's jewel,' the consul said. 'The king stole it.'

Kala was still hugging her father.

'Sir—' Daniel said.

'Morrithar, please,' the consul interrupted.

'Morrithar?'

'My name is Morrithar Nost.'

'Well, Morrithar, my name's Daniel, and I wanted to say, I am sorry I took the jewel—'

'*Stole.*'

'*Stole* the jewel, but I need it as a portal generator part to help me get home, so if we find it and the other generator parts, please may I borrow it to help open the portal? It wouldn't take long.'

Kala looked up at her father's face. The consul stood tall, and though in chains he had a more confident air than the Delvidran king.

'I thank you, Daniel, and my dear, sweet Kala,' he said, 'for freeing me from capture. I agree to your request, on one condition: if by some luck we overpower the king's guards, you and your friends shall not kill the king, but hand him over to me. I will take him to Jassk, to meet the justice of the city.'

'I agree, and shall tell my friends when we get out of here. Kala, help me search!' Daniel said.

'There is no need,' said the consul. 'I saw the captain place the jewel in the chest over there in the corner. The other parts of the machine you mention may be with it.'

The consul indicated towards a large chest with metal rivets, the chain that linked his wrists swinging back and forth, singing an eerie tune. The chest had been placed between two beds covered with the same white-and-red patterned sheets.

Daniel's heart was in his mouth. With Kala's help, he lifted the lid and bent over to look inside. They were all there! He lifted out the rubber belt he had won from Lord Phorm and placed it across his shoulder, then the backpack containing the large green jewel, which he gave to Kala.

'Keep it safe for us until you have used it to reach your home,' Kala said.

She handed the backpack back to Daniel. He put the final machine part, the box generator, in the backpack below the jewel. Daniel closed the pack, slung it over his shoulder, and, pistol outstretched in hand, led Kala and her father through the cabin doors.

Chapter 17

THE OARGRIND SEA

As they emerged onto the deck, it began to rain. The sea air was heavy, like a coat Daniel's mum had once bought and forced him to wear even though it was too big for him. He wrapped the oiled rag Ketch had given him across his flintlock's closed pan, tying it tightly. Ahead of them, almost at the main mast, the king and captain, together with the five remaining Delvidran soldiers, were attacking the three Jasskians. Daniel had no idea how twenty or so guards who had escorted the consul onto the ship had managed to see off almost forty Delvidran troops. His Uncle James would have been impressed.

Alpona was standing next to the Jasskians, a long red gash across her shoulders. Still, she was dodging sword hacks, slashes and spear lunges, and kicking with her back legs, trying to connect with faces and chests. Gripping his pistol's handle, Daniel hoped that now he would prove himself to be half as courageous as her.

'Follow me to the rowboats,' he said to Kala and her father.

They nodded, and started running past the motionless Radiant in the deck's stern-end starboard corner and along the edge of the deck.

'Daniel! Kala!' Alpona shouted.

'See you at the meeting point!' Daniel shouted back.

Alpona looked at the Jasskians struggling beside her and kicked at the Delvidran soldiers.

'Captain, get them!' the king growled mid-parry. 'They have the consul and the machine parts. I want them alive, apart from the traitor. He is mine.'

'Yes, sir,' the captain said.

While running, Daniel checked his flintlock was ready. One of the Jasskian soldiers ran across the deck to stop the captain. Slashing at her with his sword, the captain parried, spun around and stabbed with her own. The sword point glanced off the soldier's metal breastplate. The Jasskian attacked again, but the captain ducked his blade and sliced at the soldier's unarmoured thigh, causing him to fall to the deck with a cry. Daniel aimed at the captain's raised sword arm, waited for a clear shot and pulled the trigger. The pistol's hammer struck the frizzen, but despite the oiled rag across the pan, the flintlock misfired. The captain's blade swooped down, delivering the killer blow to the Jasskian soldier.

Cold rain hit Daniel's face as he squinted to see what was going on. Water sprayed onto the deck as the ship fought its way over a swell. He steadied himself, glancing back at Kala and her father. Then suddenly Daniel dropped to his knees, falling onto the deck.

'Daniel!' Kala shouted.

The captain stood behind him, smiling, her sword tip red with Daniel's blood.

'Daniel! Can you hear me?' Kala shouted.

Kala's father, his hands chained, helped her turn over Daniel's body.

'That's what happens to prisoners who think they can escape me,' the captain snarled.

Behind the captain, the rain bounced off the body of the Jasskian soldier.

'The boy's not dead, though that will leave a scar,' the captain smirked. 'My king wants him alive.'

Suddenly, Daniel opened his eyes as if shaken from a deep sleep. He touched the rubber belt across his shoulder and gripped one of the straps of his backpack.

'Once you've helped us find the queen, boy, you shall have the privilege of becoming a true Delvidran. A Radiant. I'm going to enjoy toughening you up first,' the captain said, advancing with her blade poised.

Kala's father pounced on the captain, knocking her sideways onto the deck. They wrestled in a violent embrace, the consul blocking the captain's bloody blade with his chains. Kala jumped in, trying to hold the captain's sword arm back. Getting to his feet, the consul, with help from his daughter, pushed the captain against the edge of the deck.

The captain spat and leapt at Kala, blade raised.

Alpona's hoof connected with the captain's helmet, knocking her head hard on the gunwale. She slid down, her back propping her body up against the side of the ship, legs strewn across the deck.

'That's for Lokash and the Phibs,' Alpona said to the captain's crumpled body. 'Are you okay?' she asked Daniel.

His eyes were open and he tried to say something, but the words wouldn't come. Seated on Alpona's back, clutching her mane, was Ketch, pistol aimed at the captain. He slid off her back onto his good leg, never taking his aim off the captain's body. Kala threw the captain's sword into the sea.

Kala, Ketch and the consul sat Daniel up against the side of the rowboat. He was in agony from the wound on his shoulder.

'Let's lower a rowboat; the consul's soldiers will join us shortly,' Ketch said.

'You left them?' the consul said.

'To save Daniel,' Alpona said.

'Do not worry,' Ketch said, 'I'll help them hold off the Delvidrans until the rest of you are away from the ship. We'll join you as soon as we are able.'

'How are you going to help them? You can't even walk,' the consul said.

'No, but I can stand, more or less. Now help me with that lanyard.'

Using the ropes attached by pulleys suspended above the rowboats, Ketch and the consul, with Kala's help, lifted the rowboat near the starboard side up and past the gunwale and fixed the pulley so that the boat was held level with the edge of the ship.

'I'm sorry for what happened to your friend, Ayelet Szor,' the consul said. 'I knew that the Delvidrans would torture her, and I'm so ashamed to say that I did not try to stop them.

Now she is dead, and I share the blame. I was so fixed on finding my daughter that I didn't think of others.'

'Now isn't the time,' Ketch said. 'Get in the rowboat, and I'll lower you down.'

The consul and Kala dragged Daniel into the rowboat. Alpona placed a hoof gingerly inside, testing its strength. Eventually, she decided to take the risk. Daniel's vision was blurred by the rain, but his grogginess was fading. Scratching one of the backpack straps with his left hand and touching the rubber belt with his right, he looked up at Ketch, holding the lowering rope.

'How will you and the soldiers get to the boat?' he asked, finding his voice once more.

Ketch smiled. 'I'm glad you're asking questions again. 'We'll work that out. Ready the oars.'

He lowered the rowboat into the black sea. It could fit twenty rowers, yet tossed and turned on the choppy water like a matchstick. Alpona snorted, frightened. Ketch let go of the ropes and turned towards the Delvidrans, taking a pistol from inside his jacket. Daniel watched him cover the flintlock's pan with an oily cloth strap, lift his arm and fire.

Kala and the consul struggled to put one set of the rowboat's many pairs of oars in rowlocks near the front of the boat. They asked Alpona to move to the back. Daniel tried to stand and help, but his knees buckled beneath him.

What happened next did so in a flash. Daniel heard Ketch shouting to the Jasskian soldiers left fighting the king and his remaining bodyguards and then saw him dive overboard. Two Jasskian soldiers ran after him, took off their metal helmets and armour, and also dived into the water. Through the percussion of icy rain on the rough sea, a beam of white fire thundered across the deck and over the gunwale, followed by another two splashes in the water. The two soldiers swam over to where Ketch had jumped in.

The consul held the oars from falling out of their locks. With Kala's help, Daniel managed to lift himself onto a seat on one of the thwarts.

The Jasskian soldiers who had dived overboard found Ketch and helped him swim to the rowboat. As they pulled him onto the back and across thwarts towards the middle, Daniel could see in the moonlight that the cloth covering Ketch's leg was now soaked a dark red.

'Ketch, are you okay?' he asked.

'I'll live.'

'Can you set the coordinates for Closeburn, Dumfriesshire in Scotland on Earth? You know where that is, right?' Daniel asked, taking the backpack and rubber belt off and pushing them towards him.

'I'll try, Daniel,' Ketch said.

Ketch dragged himself up onto a thwart and took the backpack and black rubber belt. He took out the box generator and set it on the thwart he had been sitting on. He fitted the rubber belt on the metallic spokes on the generator's side, then placed the green jewel in the hole designed for it on the front control panel. Daniel watched as Ketch pushed a series of buttons and pulled a few levers. The box generator began to charge with energy, then shot out a faint blue-ringed circle of blackness that stopped chest-height in the air around three feet ahead of the box. Daniel looked into the blackness within the wormhole. The portal was expanding, its blue ring opening out towards the edges of the rowboat.

Two more splashes came from the sea.

'Look!' Alpona said, her tail swishing.

Pointing her ears in the direction of the warship, she snorted. More splashes came from the water between them and the warship. The storm was picking up, and with each drop of rain on his face and down the back of his neck, Daniel felt more awake.

'Get ready! The Delvidrans are trying to board!' Kala

shouted. 'Father, let me help.'

'Storodar! Artos!' the consul shouted through the wind to the two Jasskian guards. 'Stop anyone who reaches this boat. We stand here together, men, for Jassk!' he bellowed.

'For Jassk!' the two soldiers shouted, pulling their swords from their scabbards.

They moved to the back of the boat, one on each side of Alpona. Four hands grabbed onto the back of the boat, and the first head popped up from the foam of the raging sea. Alpona turned round and lashed out with her back legs. Two hands let go. The next one was trickier. Out of the waves a spear stabbed at Alpona, grazing her leg.

She grunted, ears back. The two Jasskians hacked at the rising Delvidran soldier, who parried their blows and delivered his own until one of the Jasskian swords bit into his unprotected side and he fell forwards onto the floor of the boat.

Next came the captain, even faster without her armour. Spinning in a flurry of sword strikes, droplets of water flying from her blade, she pushed Alpona and the Jasskians back. The king then rose from the sea, tall and terrible even without his white and gold armour. The captain threw a pair of darts from a pouch on her belt into the soldiers' uncovered necks. They slid down, lost. Alpona kicked with her good leg, but the captain sprang across the boat, pressing the sword point against the horse's neck. Drawing the long, wavy dagger with her other hand, the captain shouted for the consul and Kala to get to the back of the boat. Kala scowled, but she and her father left the oars and obeyed. The king passed them, striding towards Ketch, and Daniel heard the thuds of fists hitting stomachs. Ketch fell back onto the boat's floor. The king said nothing, and held out his hand. From her belt, the captain thrust a wiry rope into his hand. The woman's sword point nicked the skin on the back of Alpona's neck. The captain eyed the consul and Kala in the back of the boat. In a flash, the king pulled Ketch from the boat's floor and threw the wire over his head. Before Ketch could lift his hands up to catch it, the king was pulling the wire tight against his throat.

'You will no longer be a nuisance to your former home, traitor,' the king said, tightening the rope.

Daniel looked back at the portal, which had stopped expanding and was now the size of the one he had gone through in the park near his home.

'I am enjoying this,' the king said with glee. 'The exile, slipping away in my hands.'

Ketch gasped for breath, trying to kick the king with his bad leg, his face becoming expressionless. Daniel looked longingly into the portal, and then turned towards the king. With no powder left, he threw his flintlock hard, striking the king's head. The king released Ketch, ripped the jewel from the machine and the blue-ringed portal shrank and vanished. He leapt at Daniel, dagger in hand. The king stopped short with a groan, his body contorting into a twisted shape. The dagger and green jewel slipped from his hands, falling into the waves. He hunched forwards, grabbed the box generator and stumbled over the side.

'No!!' Daniel shouted.

The jewel and the box generator were gone, taken by the deep. The king's motionless body floated for a moment, rocked by the violent waves. Too weak to swim against the downward pull of his scabbard belt, he slipped beneath the blackness. Ketch staggered over a thwart, almost tripping, still holding a dagger wet with the king's blood in one hand, and a flintlock as a club in the other. As the captain flew at him, Alpona stepped over the boat's thwarts.

'Duck!' she shouted.

Ketch dipped under the sword slash just in time and Alpona rose high over the captain, bringing her front hooves down on the woman's unarmoured chest. As Alpona pinned her to the floor, Ketch brought the butt of the flintlock down on her exposed head.

Chapter 18

THINKING OF PANCAKES

Daniel was in the inn's kitchen, chatting with Korel about why she didn't like horses and eating freshly baked cookies from the oven. The smell made him think of his mum in the kitchen making pancakes.

They had turned up in Forjan three days ago, their prisoner walking ahead of them, clothes torn and dirty from the dusty hike from where they had come ashore, and Korel and Jhor had shown them as much kindness as if they were their oldest, closest friends. Apart from Alpona, whom Korel had refused entry, despite Jhor's protests that it would offend 'a Sacred'.

Kala and her father had left the day before, saying they would travel home to Jassk. Apparently, they'd give the desert a miss this time. They would take the Shardspine Road, which passed around the southern edge of the Beam Wall. Daniel thought it strange without the nagging and joking. The seven Jasskian soldiers who had remained in port to tend the horses would act as their escort. Kala got her own horse for the journey, and they took nineteen riderless horses with them.

Consul Nost's radio communicator had been taken from him on the warship, so he had sent a message to the council ministers via the Mayor of Forjan's radio tower two days ago. He ordered them to send a platoon of soldiers to meet them at the Jasskian fort at the southern edge of the Beam Wall and help escort them back to the city.

On the way back to Forjan, Ketch had broken the chains around the consul's wrists with a rock, and the consul had gifted a mare each to Daniel and Ketch for their journey onwards. Alpona was very grateful, since it meant she did not have to carry Daniel and Ketch on her back any more. Kala's father had also said he would issue an official apology throughout Jassk for the accusations the Jasskian government had made towards Ketch.

Nost had told them they were always welcome in Jassk, and not to worry about the loss of his wife's jewel. He felt it had reminded him and Kala of the painful memory that she wasn't with them, and it was time to let it go. Daniel felt a lump in his throat. If he had protected the portal machine, the king would never have grabbed the jewel, or the generator. *What's done is done*, he thought. He would have to find a new jewel and a new generator. Ketch had told him he could build one with the right materials.

Jhor popped his head round the door from the bar.

'Korel, stop baking and put your cook's hat on; four specials and two cronfish mains! Five argolocs as well. And a side of sea vegetables.'

'*Chef's* hat!' Korel shot back. 'This new holiday the

mayor has created in her name is good for business, for sure. Doesn't leave much time to practise my baking skills. You'd best amuse yourself, Daniel; go see that jumped-up horse or something.'

'Alpona's really not so bad,' Daniel said.

'Take those apples with you. No use her starving her precious self. The others, too. If you're going to talk with Ketch after, then I'll bring you some dinner when I've got a moment. Not that that Delvidran woman deserves it ...'

'Korel, you're a lifesaver.' Daniel smiled.

He picked up a basket containing an assortment of small green and red apples and left the kitchen through a back door. Above him the sky was so clear, the night air cool and still. Altinor's moon was full and innumerable stars flickered as if they knew he was there, millions of miles out into space. He knew Earth was so far away, but in that moment it had never felt closer. He wondered if it was night-time in Closeburn and if his mum and sister were looking up at the same stars.

He missed his friends too, Rob, Dean and Jamie. They probably would fumble through to survive here, like him, if they had gone through the portal in the park.

Daniel walked on and came to a set of open-air pens containing livestock for the inn. He saw Alpona pacing within one of the largest pens on the side of the structure. The two mares the consul had given them were there too, watching her. Daniel lifted the basket over the fence and climbed into the pen.

'Here are some apples,' he said. 'Korel didn't want you and those new friends of yours going hungry.'

'Well, that was indeed kind of her,' Alpona said, her tail swishing in the pungent air. 'These ladies aren't so bad. A bit quiet, but I suppose that's to be expected. It's been a hard few nights with the hooligans over there, though,' she continued, tossing her head towards the loud animals in the next pen.

'It's a shame about Korel ... We'll be heading to Delvidran soon.'

'About time, if you ask me,' Alpona said. 'Telling them their king is dead, how he died, his captain our prisoner – it'll be interesting.'

'That's one word for it. Alpona, was Ayelet Szor from Delvidran?'

'You'll have to ask Ketch. He was the one who really knew her.'

Alpona dipped her head into the basket, munching on the apples. The two other smaller horses edged up and she let them in to have their fill.

'How come you didn't go through the portal when you had the chance?' she asked.

'I wanted to, so badly. But the king was going to kill Ketch and you were hurt. I couldn't just leave.'

'I'm proud of you, Daniel. If you hadn't distracted the

265

king, Ketch would have died, Kala and the consul would have become his hostages and I would have probably tried to kill myself rather than be their slave. I know what it's like to miss family. It hurts so much, sometimes it feels like your heart is shrinking inside you. I want to find my family, if any of them are still alive. I guess I just never had the nerve to cross the Broken Waste. But one day, sooner rather than later, I will. We'll find the material to build a new portal generator and get another of those gemstones to power it. Ketch and I will make sure of it.'

'Despite my initial doubts about you and Ketch, without you I wouldn't even know how to get back home.'

'So we're friends now, huh?' Alpona snorted.

'Of course.' Daniel smiled.

'We're not that bad, really,' Alpona smiled.

'You and Ketch can be pretty silly when you argue. Someone has to tell you to pack it in,' Daniel said with cheeky smile.

'I told you, we have very different leadership styles.'

Daniel laughed.

'You'd better go and see that old reprobate,' Alpona said. 'Watching the captain all day every day must be driving him mad. I'm going to show these ladies how to shut this ignorant rabble up.'

Daniel checked the basket was empty, grabbed it and made his way back to the kitchen. Dropping the basket inside, he and Korel exchanged a smile while she dashed from frying pan to bubbling pot. He went up the stairs at the side of the kitchen and pushed his way through the first door on the landing.

'How's the leg?' he asked.

'Better,' Ketch said. 'Walked around the room today. Korel did a good job patching everyone up.'

'And the prisoner?'

'Could be worse. When she gets annoying I have to gag her, though.'

Ketch was sitting on one of two beds in the small room, still wearing his now frayed jacket, one hand on a flintlock resting on the duvet, aimed at the captain. That hadn't changed in the three days they had had the dubious pleasure of her company. The captain had been gagged for part of the journey back to Forjan. Ketch rode on Alpona's back on account of his leg. Kala had changed the makeshift dressing every so often using scraps of clothing and had dressed Daniel's shoulder wound too. They had made the captain walk ahead of them, and when she'd dropped her sword and dagger on the rowboat, Ketch had encouraged her to move on. Kala had shown them which berries they could eat along the scrubland shore, but the captain had refused to eat anything until they got to Forjan.

'She sleeping?' Daniel asked.

'Looks like it.'

'I was just feeding the horses, and I asked Alpona about Ayelet Szor. She said to ask you, as you're the one who really knew her.'

For a moment Ketch stopped looking at the captain and glanced over at him. Daniel saw that the green digits of the currency display on Ketch's wrist still read twelve zeroes. He didn't think he would ever get used to the fact that people had their bank accounts embedded in their arms.

'She did, did she? What do you want to ask me?'

'She could be listening,' Daniel whispered, looking at the captain.

'It doesn't matter what she hears now. She's coming back to Delvidran with us. After we tell them what she and Ordran have done, it will be up to the people of Delvidran what happens to her. Nothing she hears from us will help her cause.'

Daniel noticed Ketch was no longer calling Ordran 'king'.

'Was Ayelet from Delvidran?'

'She worked there for a time, but was from somewhere else.'

'If she knew about portal technology like you, maybe she had travelled to Earth at some stage, and maybe she left some machine parts or another generator in her house—'

'Daniel, I promise you, we will find a way to get you home,' Ketch interrupted. 'Ayelet was a prodigious inventor, and Collector for Ao Sirt's council at one point. We developed the technology together to travel to other worlds. She was once my closest friend ... We'll build a new stardeath generator, and find a power source even if we have to build a submarine to find the green jewel that Ordran carelessly dropped into the ocean.' He smiled faintly.

'Ayelet sounded like quite a person. I wish we could have stopped—'

'There was no way we could have stopped her torture or illness.' Ketch swallowed. 'Ordran and Laton did this, no one else.'

Daniel knew that he meant the captain. At least now he knew the name of the person who had hunted him down.

'Alpona really wants to search for her family. I just don't get Korel's attitude towards horses.'

'Good thing for her we're leaving tomorrow then. I've been thinking of a method to help Alpona cross the Broken Waste with water to drink. Let's talk about it after we reach Delvidran.'

'There is the plan for finding your wife, too.'

'Yup, I know.'

'It was kind of Ayelet to leave you her house in her will.'

'I wish I could bring her back ... I'll repair her house and look through her papers, see what she was working on. It'll wait until after Delvidran, though. When the mayor told me that Ayelet had written a will before she got ill, she said she'd have the Town Watch keep an eye on the house. She may have hunted sea beasts in her past career, but that old lady is all right.'

'It was interesting that the consul didn't mention the loss of his wife's jewel when describing the fight at sea.'

'Indeed,' Ketch agreed. 'The mayor is itching to launch a salvage operation on the warship. I don't think Consul Nost wants them looking for a jewel.'

He pointed at the captain with his gun.

'Spending some quality time with her makes me think of the Radiants. They only function when commanded by Ordran or Laton. They probably made more of them in Delvidran, so that's another thing to sort out. Separating each person from the machine they are imprisoned in is one thing, waking them from their comas quite another.'

'We'll find a way. You wouldn't be much of an engineer if a few Radiants stopped you.'

'You know the Radiants were based on my own designs,' Ketch said. '*She* altered them.' Ketch sighed, looking at the prisoner. 'Added the people, and the symbiotic relationship between them and the machines. Created them as an unstable weapon rather than a tool for heavy lifting.'

'Well, perhaps she can help us *un*create them.'

'I wouldn't bet on it. I fear the four Radiants that went into the sea may have succumbed to the water pressure. The Oargrind Sea is pretty deep, even near the coastline.'

Daniel paused.

'I can't imagine what it would be like to become a Radiant. The captain said—'

'Laton!' Ketch interjected. 'She was Ordran's captain. He is dead.'

'She said she would make me into a Radiant after I had helped guide them around Earth.'

'An honourable fate, according to her. Virtually everyone else on Altinor thinks otherwise.'

'What are we going to do with her? Going back to the castle with the news that we have killed their king and have his Captain of the Guard prisoner may not go down as well as you'd hope.'

'I'll make sure she gets justice in Delvidran. We'll tell them of the dubious things she and Ordran did, why I had to kill him, and suggest a trial for Laton. You are right, some people of Delvidran, mainly those in the military, will not be happy. With Ordran leaving no children, and no clear successor from among his family or Delvidran's other noble families, wouldn't it be nice to have elections?' Ketch smiled.

'You will never convince the people to abandon the monarchy,' Laton said, her eyes glaring. 'The royal family of Natos have ruled Delvidran for centuries. Who are you to try to change what the people want?'

A menace even in chains, Daniel thought.

'The Natos family lost the goodwill of the Delvidrans

271

when they began treating their people like slaves, putting them in killing machines and invading other people's lands for their own ends,' Ketch replied.

'You shall see,' Laton said. 'A successor shall be agreed. In the end, you are simply another piece of rabble-rousing filth, stuck to the boot of Delvidran. And we will pick you off. Perhaps the fact that you will never see her again has made you forget that, as a Delvidran, you are the subject and servant of Ordran's successors until your death.'

Ketch jumped at her, wrapping a gag from his pocket around her mouth.

'We'll find your wife,' said Daniel. 'The soldiers are the main concern in Delvidran. Who knows how they will react?'

'I know I will find her,' Ketch said. 'Regarding the soldiers, well, we'll just have to convince them of a different way forward.'

Korel pushed open the door, carrying a huge tray containing a tankard of water, three glasses and three plates of fish, colourful vegetables and something that looked like black mashed potato.

'Can't have you starving,' she said, laying the tray down on the bedside table near Ketch.

'That looks great.' Ketch beamed. 'Thank you, my dear Korel, you are too kind.'

'Kinder than whoever made your jacket, that's for sure,' she joked.

'Ha–ha, I made it myself. You've never seen anything like it.'

'I'll take your word for it. Sure won't win any beauty contests in this neck of the woods.'

'With Alpona in the pens, Ketch misses being made fun of.' Daniel smiled.

'Well, she's there for a reason. My inn, my rules. If there's anything else you'll be wanting, let me know. I'll be in the kitchen tending to the unexciting dietary needs of our clientele. Nothing like food to help the mind and provide ballast for more drinks.'

She winked, and left the room.

Ketch sighed. 'I'll have to remove the gag again.'

The next morning, Forjan was unusually quiet. The mayor, busy with events for the Mayor's Holiday, which happened to coincide with their return to Forjan, had sent a note to wish them a safe trip. Alpona had stressed to Daniel her wish to leave before dawn, and both he and Ketch had agreed. Most of the residents weren't awake yet. They packed the food and bottles of water Korel had given them, placing them in saddlebags over the mares' backs. Daniel and Ketch then mounted their rides, and, flintlock in hand, Ketch encouraged Laton, still chained and gagged, to sit in front of him on his horse. The scowl on her face as she sat in the saddle made Daniel feel apprehensive.

Alpona trotted around the group, neighing in the direction of the pens. Daniel thought there was a hint of acknowledgement to the other animals and he smiled. She even mustered enough goodwill to neigh goodbye to Korel and Jhor. Daniel and Ketch shouted farewell to their hosts, and as Alpona and Ketch's mare set off, Daniel lightly squeezed his legs against the sides of his own horse and loosened the reins. The horse stepped forward, and he looked round at Korel and Jhor, smiled and gave them a wave. He wondered if he would ever see them again. He would never forget them and their kindness, or that of Niya and her husband at the hotel in Jassk.

The sun was beginning to rise over the Oargrind Sea, creating shadows that stretched out ahead of them. They cantered along the dusty track that marked the beginning of the Thrakos Road to Delvidran.

Daniel clasped the metal symbol on the chain around his neck. He had thought of his mum constantly, even his sister, and never more so than in the last few days. The voice he had heard back at home in Closeburn that night, which said it knew about his father, had also been on his mind. Did Altinor have some link to his family? He had to find out.

'Now that we're on our way,' Alpona said, turning back to draw level with Daniel and Ketch on the other horses, 'I can tell you the full story of how I escaped capture from that woman and her Radiants.'

'Thought you already did,' Ketch groaned, grinning.

'I think we have time to hear it again,' Daniel smiled. He thought Alpona's story would take his mind off thinking about Mum and Rachel. He didn't even care now that his sister always got pancakes first.

Thank you for reading *Closeburn Crossing*, the first novel in the *Altinor* trilogy. Gaining exposure as an independent author relies mostly on word-of-mouth, so if you have the time and inclination, please consider leaving a short review wherever you can.

GLOSSARY

Altinor — another world, far from Earth

altins — Altinorean form of currency

Ao Sirt — an Altinorean state ruled from a city of the same name

Arloth — a river in Shard

Beam Wall — a wall of lethal energy at least four hundred feet high created by the Jasskians to keep desert raiders out of the Jassk City's supporting farmlands

biotricity — a form of energy, similar to electricity but more targetable and with less conductivity

Broken Waste — an immense wasteland in Shard dominated by an active volcano, Tephr

Collector — a type of engineer and inventor. Many governments on Altinor appoint at least one Collector to work for them

Chorozon — name of King Ordran's flagship

Delvidran — an Altinorean kingdom ruled from a castle town of the same name

Dran — Shard's greatest river

Forjan — a large port town

Forjan firewater — a heady Forjanian drink

Iria — Shard's greatest jungle

Itta — a forest

Jassk — an Altinorean state ruled from a large city of the same name

Jasskian strong-ale — a Jasskian ale

korcite — a metallic material found on Altinor

Kotorr — a continent on Altinor, smaller than Shard

Melithusa — a goddess worshipped by some on Altinor

Modner gang — a gang based in Forjan

monitorvisor — a Jasskian device with a screen, similar to Earth's television

Mornaren — the name of the castle in Delvidran town

Oargrind Sea — a sea on Altinor, smaller than the Sea of Melithusa

Phib — a large bipedal talking frog. Phibs live in Iria and have a warrior culture

Phibia — a large village in Iria, capital of the Phibs

Port of Delvidran — a port some miles south of Delvidran which serves Delvidran town

Radiants — hulking machines, weapons of war, each have a coma-induced being trapped within, their biotricity fuelling the machine and acting as its ammunition

repair mecha — a robot used to repair broken bones and accelerate the healing time of injuries

Rusted Station — a hover-train station north of Iria

Sea of Melithusa — a sea on Altinor

Searcher — a flying robot, resembling a large hawk in size and appearance, used to hunt beings

Shard — a large continent on Altinor

stardeath generator — machine used to create portals to points in universes

Tephr — an enormous active volcano in Shard

"The Sacred" — an early name given by some to the one known tribe of horses that speak

"The Shields" — an ancient warrior family from lands in the mountains beyond Ao Sirt. Some of them and their descendants have the ability to create force fields with their minds which protect them from physical and mental attack

whistberry — a type of Altinorean berry which grows in clusters on shrubs

whistberry sherb — a potent green drink made from whistberries

zaffer clarsact — a Jasskian drink made from Altinorean blue lemons and honey

ACKNOWLEDGEMENTS

My thanks and appreciation go out to my family and friends for their encouragement and support. Not least to my mum and dad and my grandparents, whose gifts of stories and experiences showed me the importance and joy of exploring the imagination.

Thanks as well to Sarah Cheeseman, whose editing helped shape this book.

Thanks also to Nathan Mckenna, who created amazing cover art, and his agent Alice Ball.

Last, but far from least, all my love and gratitude to my beautiful wife Arleta, who created the map with me, edited the manuscript and without whom the process of writing this book would have been a great deal less enjoyable.

About the Author

Giles J.M. Blackley has written articles and short stories for a number of magazines, e-book distributors and travel websites including Smashwords and 'History of Britain Magazine'. *Closeburn Crossing*, book one in the *Altinor* trilogy, is his first novel. He lives in Edinburgh with his wife and Monty the cat.

You can follow Giles on Facebook @gilesjmblackley and visit his website gilesjmblackley.com.

Read more about Altinor in the upcoming book two in the *Altinor* trilogy

25496516R00169

Printed in Poland
by Amazon Fulfillment
Poland Sp. z o.o., Wrocław